YORAM KANIUK

# BETWEEN LIFE AND DEATH

*Translated from the Hebrew*
*by Barbara Harshav*

RESTLESS BOOKS
BROOKLYN, NEW YORK

First Restless Books hardcover edition September 2016

ISBN: 9781632060921
Library of Congress Control Number: 2016939493

Cover design by Strick and Williams Design
Set in Garibaldi by Tetragon, London

Ellison, Stavans, and Hochstein LP
232 3rd Street, Suite A111
Brooklyn, NY 11215
www.restlessbooks.com

publisher@restlessbooks.com

# BETWEEN LIFE AND DEATH

AFTER THESE THINGS—after disease and after death and after pain and after laughter and after betrayal and after old age and after grace and love and after a foolish son the heaviness of his mother and a woman of valor who stayed with me in beauty in the abyss—after all that I woke up into a half sleep and stayed there four months. And it was bad and it was good and it was sad and it was lost and it was a miracle and it was what it was and it wasn't what it wasn't and it could have been and I recalled it was night. A night sealed up in its night. I spent it in bad dreams and woke up dazed with sleep, I was healthy, in my house at 13 Bilu Street, and suddenly I recalled that at night I'd dreamed of screwdrivers. I had no need of a screwdriver and so I didn't search and I didn't find it, but in the place where the screwdriver could have been if there had been one, I found an old map of Tel Aviv, and since the map was already there, I left it and went to drink coffee and I ate a croissant they call *corasson* here and returned home, to the map, and thought of looking for the street where I lived. I spread the map on the

7

table and wandered around with my finger until it landed, but not on Bilu Street, where I live, and not on the nearby corner of Balfour and Rothschild Boulevard, where I lived my first three years, but on the Arlozorov corner of Eduard Bernstein, near the place where I really grew up. Naturally, I had no choice but to go to the corner of Arlozorov and Bernstein, where, except for the days when I walked in the sands, I passed by for eight years, ten months a year, almost every morning, walking from my parents' house to the Model School and back—a distance in which I could, if I wanted, get to the moon.

At the street corner, which was ugly even back then, stood the wretched house where Agu lived. He was two years younger but older than me, and was taciturn, scorned, solitary, and full of hate. I think he stayed in third grade for three years, or maybe that was somebody else, and he had sparkling brown eyes and he was killed in the war in a battle for Neve Samuel soon after he ran into me in the dining hall of Kibbutz Kiryat Anavim, when he recalled who I was even before I reminded him where we knew each other from. We were then digging graves before the battles, and all you had to do was return from the battle and bury, and since only I knew who Agu was, I was asked to write his name in a florid hand, but I didn't know his real name, only his nickname, Agu, and I didn't know if, when he was born, he had even had a name, and in fact I have no idea if he was even born, and I recall him as somebody who had been here forever, maybe because the Muslim graveyard flowing down to his house on the corner of Arlozorov Street was so close.

Agu's father had a bicycle-repair shop on the corner of Jabotinsky, which was called Ingathering of the Exiles Street back then. The exiles didn't manage to be gathered in, but they've already forgiven Jabotinsky and changed the name of the street to his name, and that's how the names changed. His dog, Topsy, would run to The Tribes of Israel Street from the other side of Keren Kayemet Boulevard to attack the composer von Sternberg, whom he loathed. The composer would walk around dressed even on weekdays in a German hunter's outfit and would brandish a bamboo walking stick and look frightening with his eyes shut and was married to Genia, a beautiful woman who was my first love and who brought up her son and became a nun in Lebanon. Sternberg the putz wrote a work that three people in the city could listen to without killing themselves and called it "Twelve Tribes of Israel," after the name of his street, and Moshe my father said we were lucky he didn't live in Meah Shearim, with its hundred gates.

I used to play with the dog Topsy on the way to school, and Agu was mad at his dog for wagging his tail at me, and he was jealous of me and yelled at Topsy, but Topsy was fond of me and sensed that I liked him and waited for me every morning with his tail wagging, until one day Agu got upset and jealous and sicced Topsy on me and yelled at him to bite me. Topsy, who belonged to Agu but loved me, tried in panic to bite Agu but then was kicked and his tail drooped and his eyes raged and he whined horribly and approached me and Agu shrieked again and Topsy didn't know where his greater obligation was and bit me because he had no choice. Poor Topsy was taken to the veterinary department for tests and I had to get twenty shots in my stomach. I went with Sarah my mother to the Strauss Clinic on Balfour Street and they'd give me a shot every week with a giant needle and after my portion of torments, we'd leave there, go down to Allenby Street, and Sarah my mother would buy me an ice cream at Shnir and call it "some consolation" for what I had gone through.

Agu's father has been gone a long time. Not only him. All of them have gone with the wind. Even the watchmaker Yashka Silberman, who taught Stalin Yiddish, has gone, and Goldbaum, the barber from Warsaw licensed for men and women, whose wife ran away from him wearing a corset and he was afraid to run after her because of the Italian planes that were bombing and because he was wearing a gas mask and couldn't get it off, he's gone, too, and the shoemaker Joshua, who taught me to cut soles and spit nails in an arc into a sole, is gone, and the limping upholsterer Yashke Weisman, who was killed in an accident and his wife married her lover, and Mr. Polishuk, who dreamed of rain in its season fell on me, and I stood shaking from the wind blowing from the sea and I was excited, but I don't remember why. Maybe because I grew up woven into that sea and the melody was in me. I'd sit in the dark on the veranda, back then we called it a porch, and like most of the residents of our city I'd peep in the windows of the neighbors to see how they were creating the Hebrew soldiers of the future. Years ago, long before I got sick and before I was transferred a little to the other side, years when I dreamed of growing old and dying at the sea, with the strong wind and the taste of salt in my mouth, because that was what was always here, the surest future was the sea. I thought that if I got sick, and back then I wasn't really sick, and if I lay dying at the sea and I listened to the singing of the wind, I would love my death.

I stood at the corner of Eduard Bernstein Street and looked up. The veranda we had, the small panorama to the sea, was hidden long ago by tall buildings, and the sea was hidden by big, indescribably ugly buildings. But I can still picture on the veranda next to ours, where even now you can see a little bit of sea, the poor Lichtman maiden, may she rest in peace, standing strong and weeping like a captain on the bridge of a sinking ship, and even though she died years ago, she's still holding the telescope she was sold by the black-market egg seller, Mr. Bein, who carried the eggs in a small splendid suitcase, always dressed in a suit and tie he said he'd brought, in his words, from Berlin—and she stands and looks out sadly at Germany, and sees those who were her parents in Berlin, and tells us, foolish children that we were, who at the age of eight were already training to establish a Jewish state, which was impossible but essential in hostile regions, and getting ready to take revenge on the Nazis with slingshots and sticks—she tells us she saw what was what before they made soap of them, and every hour she takes the razor blades out of the case and shaves, and between one shave and another you can see her beard sprouting, bursting from her cheeks like flowers after the first rain, and she'd search for her father even in the fuse box and explain that he had to be someplace, so why not there, and she'd say that it was all from the Holocaust, and she missed Germany so much that she'd sing sweet lieder to the sea, though she had no voice at all, so that it would take her back, and I told my friend Amos, who would come see her beard grow, I told him she wanted to swim to Berlin, but she stayed to die in Palestine the Land of Israel, clinging like a leech to stormy regrets. For regrets gave her sweet pain, and I would cuddle up to her pain, which I almost understood, and draw it into me and it stayed in me like a guest who stays forever.

I remember the sight of the ships on the way to the port of Tel Aviv. I loved them like rocking nutshells during a storm, and I loved the whistle of the strong wind. Now I'm old and without a screwdriver, unneeded guys like me are called seniors, and I walk on Eduard Bernstein Street, with broke, but they continued to be piled up because he continued to create them until they reached the top of the lemon tree and then he cut down the lemon tree, which served as a lesson to Ashael, and so when the War of Liberation broke out in 1947, he ran off to America and a few years later was called to the US Army to fight in Korea, and his mother, who said that Ashael was both her son and a substitute for her idiotic husband, who had spent all his days building concrete boxes that looked like coffins for dwarves, flew to New York in an aeroplane, today we call it a plane, and flying was a rare thing back then, and bought somebody important in city hall with money from Ashael's father that she smuggled in her gigantic bra, and somebody arranged papers for Ashael and released him from the war.

Near the house, right across from the calm hidden beauty where I searched for a gutter to play me the lullabies of my childhood, a little bit of sea is still open. Moshe my father would swim in it every day at exactly five in the afternoon, after most of the swimmers had already gone home, because he loved having the sea all to himself. In the spring and fall, the sea was sparkling and smooth and soft, and sometimes in the morning, on the way to school, we'd walk barefoot in the sand along the shore, and under the hewn-limestone wall, we'd take off our shoes, hang them by the laces on our shoulder, put our schoolbags on our heads like the Arab women who carry ewers of water and bundles of wood to escorting a most splendid ant bearing a small canopy of dry grass, and under the canopy I saw a tiny tumor, snug as a king bug. Meanwhile, the sky cleared and the clouds went off. At the sea, the secret bays and the natural pool weren't yet murdered, and above the pool, cut in the limestone, was the secret cave with the canned goods and the rusks we hid in case Rommel won in Egypt and the Nazis conquered the Land of Israel and we had to make Masada in the cave, and we said that as in the poem, which Teacher Blich would recite excitedly and tearfully, we would build Jerusalem on the hill like those who mount the scaffold.

The son of Teacher Blood and Fire, Trumpeldor, who was said to be the most beautiful boy in our school, and who certainly joined or didn't join—I don't remember anymore—the group of "Masada rebels on the limestone," as we were called back then, stood proud, beautiful, and well built on the rock in the natural pool, and Zilpha S., who was already wearing a bra, and we knew she was wearing a bra because we'd hit the girls on the back to know and with her we felt the buttons, and there was even some slander that she once kissed someone and even danced ballroom dances, Zilpha S. said that Blood and Fire Trumpeldor looked like Tarzan on the rock, and I annoyed her when I laughed at what she said, because what little girl, even if she did wear a bra, understands Tarzan from the community center at eleven cents a movie. Afterward, I was sorry and I said he looked like a hero to me. Trumpeldor, we called him Trumpel, spread his hands, leaned forward a little like Nimrod the mighty hunter, and everybody stood amazed and applauded him. He waved his hands and waved us away with a certain contempt and raised his head and looked at me and laughed because I always made him laugh with who I was, and he shouted as always, "To Yoram, who will conquer a cloud," and then he added of course, "To Life and to Death," and stretched his hands forward and then leaned a bit more, and all of a sudden a frozen silence reigned over the face of the water and he roared like Zilpha S.'s Tarzan and rose on his tiptoes and jumped head first into the shallow water and I saw his beautiful head touch the water, hit a rock, and I heard the sharp crack and the water turned red and pieces of head were in it.

The tumor on the ants' cradle looked nervous, but detached, maybe it was searching for victims with infuriating indifference. I sensed that tumors, microbes, and ants love each other, and I thought there was some justice in that, in a world where everyone swallows everyone else. The ants were escorting the tumor under the canopy in splendid formation, and they looked as if they were part of an expedition of divine adulation. Maybe ultimately some microbe died that had clung to the tumor's body, and the ants were the only ones in this country that really maintained the friendship of the poem and were holding a proper funeral for the microbe, and so the tumor apparently came and attended his dear one's funeral. I thought that I do know tumors. I'm eaten by them. But I didn't hate them, and I looked on impressed and didn't think about the procession anymore. The next evening I went to meet the intended bride of Rebecca's son, who always walked around with an enormous rifle and found the smallest Australian woman on the continent and was about to start a family with her and the two of them together were maybe seven and a half feet tall. At the end of the evening I went back to my house on Bilu, and on my way there I came to Marmorek Street. From the corner of Ibn Gabirol stretched a line of cars toward the parking lot of the concert hall, may it rest in peace.

I'm lying now in the miracle of my life that has passed and thinking of the miracle. Of the procession of the tumor. Now I remember that I don't know how and why, how in 1945, we all went to Masada to shout "We won't forget you, Exile" and one guide, who was in the Palmach, shot a bullet from a gun he had hidden on him and I marched onto the crest, it was Hanukkah and cold and dark, and I looked out and in that whole landscape there were lights like a giant Christmas because the blackout of the great war was lifted and I thought that what I was seeing was the Garden of Eden, sparkling and beautiful, but I felt shocked and I heard a stone falling into an abyss, and I skipped back and I understood that I was standing on the edge of Masada and in a little while I would become a stone at the foot of the mountain, and I thought that when Jews stand on the edge, they see the Garden of Eden, and vice versa.

And here, at Marmorek, facing the line of cars, I thought about the cloud that brought rain on me at Eduard Bernstein and wandered with me, and I had no choice but to bring it here. It brought rain down on the slowly moving cars, the car windows were closed and raised a liquid scrim of sweat, and here and there what they call music today burst out of one of the windows. I stood on the traffic island between two cars. Now and then the cars crept forward a few inches and I looked for a breach to cross the street safely, and the drivers sat frozen inside the closed cars and a nerve-racking hum of tense silence was heard and I stood between two cars that stopped right at the traffic island I had to cross to get to my side of Bilu, and suddenly one of the cars burst out of the end of the line and swooped forward wildly and flew past the long line and its driver shrieked and came to the head of the line. He cut left to the opposite lane and the driver I stood behind was scared and the driver I stood in front of was also scared and I heard two shouts at the same time and the two jounced and I managed to move fast before those two cars touched one another and crushed me and from the window of the car behind me the newscaster

Haim Yavin was heard saying "no injured" and the drivers who lost control started cursing the offender.

In the morning, not far from there, near Samson's store, a black cat passed by me. He slipped from right to left or from left to right, I don't remember exactly. I thought about the microbe attached to the tumor I saw the evening before under the ant's canopy and I remembered how Moshe my father mocked our neighbors, whom he despised, because they sat on the verandas in pajamas and believed in superstitions about black cats. The miniature Russian woman with beautiful eyes who cleans our street stood at the corner of Carmiya and Bilu and walked and looked at me and spread her hands and shouted something in Russian and said I looked like a nice man, even though I was old, but nice, and I have great luck that I'm still alive after the black cat ordered my death. She crossed herself excitedly. I told her she was behaving strangely and she burst into spontaneous weeping that was so neat and nice and maybe she was mocking me, because she said, "I cleans your street and know who you are, you live in the house of Romania," and then she pulled out a photo and said that the woman in the picture was her mother, and I looked and she really did look like a beautiful young woman standing on a shaded street among dense trees on a boulevard in Odessa, and Odessa is my mother Sarah's hometown, and I told her that my mother was born in Odessa and she was glad, and I was also impressed by her language all of a sudden, maybe that was from the course, "Seven sisters together," she said and added, "Where was the lady from in Odessa?" I said that Sarah my mother wasn't a lady and came to the Land of Israel in 1909, when she was a little girl, so I'm not sure she knew her mother. The Russian woman calculated the years, muttered something, shook her head in disbelief, and said, "But how back then? There was no Israel," and I told her that was right, Israel waited for me to be born, and she smiled, apparently she thought she'd found an idiot, which wasn't far from the truth, and she said the black cat is bad luck and crosses help Jews more than Stars of David.

I told her that on the ship that I worked on in 1949 and that brought Holocaust survivors there were a lot of girls who wore crosses around their neck and said they wouldn't bring Jewish children into the world and one of them told me she would kill any Jewish child who dared sneak into her womb. I saw a tear flow from the Russian woman's left eye and I don't know why I remember that it was the left one, maybe because I'm a lefty, or as Sarah my mother used to say, left-handed, and I told her I missed the bunch of trouble destined for me from the black cat because the evening before, on the traffic island here on the corner of Marmorek, I was almost killed twice, the first time when an idiot driver galloped past me, and the second time when two cars I stood between almost crushed me, and maybe the a lot, but a yeshiva student who said he was almost a rabbi and revealed to me that he was trying to get money for an abortion for a girl forbidden to him who was pregnant and he adjusted the mezuzah, prayed over it, and kissed it as if it were a girl who needed an abortion, and prayed so devotedly that I gave him a little more money for the abortion because I thought I would help decrease the population he represented. I told the Russian woman, who listened to me with an incomprehensible excitement, that maybe all that happened precisely because my mezuzah was too kosher.

I thought, despite the death that was lurking for me twice yesterday and seemed determined to harm me, I was quite a healthy man. Old age had indeed leaped on me as it leaps on all of us, and age isn't something that showers favors and not a big holiday either, and my blood pressure is quite high, and I've got back problems and migraines, and I had a prostate operation, and once I had herpes like Golda, which was an affliction, that is both of them, the herpes and Golda, and I had a small brain incident that damaged my balance, but nothing drastic that couldn't be treated, and the evening after the encounter with the sweet Russian woman on Marmorek Street, I returned from the boulevard with my dog Adam, who pounced on a cat that climbed a tree, and I had to hold onto him hard and almost dislocated my shoulder and came home and felt pressure in my neck, a sure sign of high blood pressure. I fed Adam and looked in the drawer for medication to bring down blood pressure and found only one pill. So I needed a prescription and called Pnina, Dr. Szold's secretary, who sees patients in the clinic on Reines, and the next day I went and he examined me and gave me a prescription but also advised me to do blood and urine tests because everybody over fifty gets checked once or twice a year and he told me, "Remember you're not young anymore and three years ago you had a stroke and you're not playing football with your eyes closed," something I hadn't done even in my youth, but I thought, What's so bad about living a little longer?

The next day it cleared up and a winter sun beamed. I walked to the Maccabee clinic on Balfour Street for a blood test and a few days later, I went back to Dr. Szold, I waited in the waiting room, read a story in a two-year-old women's magazine about a girl who was born with four children in her womb, until Dr. Szold called me in, said he had checked the results in the computer and everything was fine, but was concerned about an anemia that hadn't been seen before and a colonoscopy was a good idea. I called to make an appointment. They told me that, because of my condition, they'd move my appointment up and I'd wait only two months. I wrote a rather nasty article about the long wait for an exam recommended all the time on television and in the press, and some good-hearted person read the article, called, and fixed an appointment for me in a week, I went to the doctor, he examined me, said it probably wasn't anything, and explained sound like toothpaste, but her soft white body is also like toothpaste. She smiled at me with what looked to me like love that still belonged to an age of hidden love, and the main thing is that it wasn't only pity, which was apparently in her, although she didn't emphasize it, and that annoyed me, but pleased me even more. The professor was wearing clothes different from those he wore when he gave me an enema, now he was wearing light, sporty clothes, although he was limping, apparently he himself wasn't altogether healthy, which somehow helped me. He sat in his chair and looked back and forth between me and the photo and in a velvety voice, slightly constrained but mixed with restrained force, he said quite tenderly, "I've got something to tell you." I glanced at Miranda. She looked regal in her sadness, in her blue dress, sitting very close to me on the brown sofa. She took hold of my hand and smiled at me and kept holding my hand and I was comforted and said to Professor Halperin, "Speak, for your servant hears." He tried to smile and said, "I'm sorry, we found some small polyps in the colon that aren't malignant, and of course, we destroyed them, but there is one big and quite serious polyp that may very well be malignant, and you need an operation."

I said, "Tell me when." He looked at me in amazement. After a long moment he asked how come I wasn't upset or crying. People generally cry at that moment. I told him that I had heard an announcement that I have a malignant disease in my mind so many times that now it really happened, there was no need to panic. Moshe my father used to say about people who read a lot of medical books that they were liable to die of a heart attack because of a typographical error. Halperin tried to repress a smile and looked at me sweetly and I told him that, aside from that, I was following the path of King David, who mourned until his son died and after his death got up and got dressed and ate, and I also mourned for myself before or after but not at the moment of truth. He shook my hand. He studied me. I was also amazed at how calm I was. I wasn't in any state of mind but I wasn't worried. Today it seems strange that I didn't get upset. After all, a doctor comes and says I'd have an operation to remove a cancerous growth, and instead of panicking, I suddenly wrap myself in some stupid calm, as if it were all happening to somebody else.

The next day, I went to Surgical Ward B in the hospital and they performed all the tests on me. They dragged me up and down in elevators and examined everything but my earlobe. I was photographed as if I were a fashion model. They put me in a CAT scan that looked like a gigantic cement mixer, spun the shining wheel around me while I was inside, inundated by capering lights. Finally, because of the brain incident I had had before, they also had to test the inner ear. They took me to the hospital cellar. There sat a doctor who had a Russian accent but spoke fluent Hebrew. He told me to sit down and asked me to gesture to him when I wanted to throw up or when I felt dizzy or like fainting. "This test is not considered pleasant," he said, and smiled, he really did seem to empathize with my trouble, and added in a gentle voice, "But what can we do? We've got no choice." There was concern in his voice, but also a pleasure that wasn't completely disguised. He lay me on a bed, told me to look at the ceiling, moved a few things, played with hoses, checked water pouring in an enormous stream, and I felt slightly dizzy. He brought a hose close with a round bronze spigot at the tip, and said, "Sorry, sir, this will be hard," and he started shooting into my ear a strong stream of boiling water that penetrated to my brain. Never had I seen water shooting so powerfully, except for news broadcasts when police scatter demonstrators. Here there was just a little ear, and a strong stream, and a small room, and a cellar, but I hadn't felt such pleasure in a long time. The doctor kept looking at me. He smiled. He looked amazed. I was sorry for him that I wasn't suffering because maybe that would have helped him. But he didn't say a word, put a hose in the other ear, too, streamed the water again, and it was even nicer for me. I was silent. Now he looked annoyed, checked the hoses, brought a new hose with a new spigot, shot ice water into my ear, and I smiled. Silence. I got up. He gave me a confused look, I asked him if he could arrange another visit here one, she asks one of the patients, he gives it to her, and then the doctor takes the paper and gives it to me and I sign and don't know exactly what I'm signing, and somebody pulls out the plywood strip under the pillow and Professor Clausner comes, who visited me two days before to explain to me what he would do when he slaughtered me, and he was wearing a green robe with a white mask over his mouth and he looked excited at the impending disaster.

They take me to the navel of the hall, which looks like a football field. All at once, the space is cut up and disintegrates into a lot of small cubicles and I'm inside one of them. The canvas gate is closed and I feel the strong cold stabbing me and cutting the poor microbes and me, too. I want to complain but I'm ashamed and think, Who am I when he's cut up? And then grave robbers wrapped in masks assault me and wait for me to die, and the curtains are closed, and I'm separated from the world. Something in me says the hell with it, die now, pay later, death at bargain rates, one death for ten shekels, two deaths for six. The main thing is don't make any noise. Here, they're cutting. I'm at the entrance and maybe at the exit, too. Lots of knives here. A dull noise of electronic instruments. The son of Sarah my mother is lying with his face to the lamp and hears the tumult. They're giving me injections, and the frost suits the moment, and the professor says, "Don't worry! I'm here," and I sink, for a moment. I see the professor's eyes looking past my face, quickly approaching, I want to return to my natural state, but I don't have a natural state, I'm a panicky corpse. The professor's eyes come closer and closer and then I enter an intangible and frozen oblivion, everything silenced.

I woke up in the recovery room. Apparently, hours had passed. Miranda and my daughter Naomi came in. They took the disgusting bloody gown I had worn off my stomach so I could enjoy the wonder of my new embellished belly. I look and see that it has turned into a giant illustration of big red stitches that look like an ancient map or etching, embroidered warp and woof as far as the neck like an old dried leaf, or better, like a fishbone. Professor Clausner comes solemnly, now without the mask over his mouth but his apron stained with my blood, and I know my blood and he looks like he's bleeding a little like a royal butcher. With a wise smile he says he was there, he himself operated, it wasn't an operation done by a messenger, and I should know that there was quite a big cancerous growth so we had to cut almost half of my colon and a third of the bowel, after which he explained that the cancer was on the right side of the bowel, but the operation was a success, no metastases. "In a few days," he said, "you'll go home like new."

Never before had I thought about my colon or my bowel that isn't a colon. Now that I was robbed of a third of what had been in my only belly, which I hadn't exactly loved but which was part of me, I felt that that cancer was mine. I gave birth to it. Miranda gave birth to daughters, I gave birth to cancer. When can a man enjoy what he gave birth to? I asked the professor if he remembered whether he operated on me lovingly and where they took the cancer, since my favorite writer, Mishima, wrote that to love an apple you had to get to its heart and to get to the heart of the apple, you had to murder it. He smiled painfully, as if I didn't appreciate some great work he had achieved, and told me with restrained sadness that I was lucky I came out as I did.

I lay in bed and nurses came and washed me. Miranda and Naomi stayed. I started getting better. I was in pain, but I was slightly drugged and the pains were under control. What is more, after two days there was no more "going home." My tattooed stomach, all beautifully and delicately engraved with the artistic seams, rebelled. I heard it humming and the butcher's wonderful seams burst like an eggshell. I couldn't produce urine, I felt faint and I lost consciousness. Consciousness returned and I wanted to say something, it was on the tip of my tongue, I was frantic, I started talking, no words came out and I lost consciousness again and I woke up lying on a gurney on the way back to the slaughter hall.

The gurney stopped in a doorway where a winding line of supermarket carts stood with young men and women lying in them looking frozen and wearing colorful clothes. I looked at them and thought maybe they were statues. They were stuck in contorted poses but not moving. A young woman, almost a child, dressed up for some party, in a short red dress—her legs were bent but not moving, and she, I know, and I don't know how I know, was dead, but she also apparently envied me because they were bringing me to the sacrifice before her, and she burst into tears and said why him of all people, that is, me, but the weeping didn't come out of her because after all she was dead. And then comes my daughter Naomi with the ancient Jewish beauty she inherited from her gentile mother and she caresses my face. I see how the beautiful young people, painted in splendid colors, are lost in the entrance to the enormous church of knives and Naomi holds onto me and helps the orderlies take me inside.

I'm sad for the youngsters in the carts. I think I knew they were injured in traffic accidents. They wore holiday clothes and it hurt me to see them. A plump doctor made me sign the form I don't read this time either, and the x-ray machine once again moves over me, the man above smiles at me like an old acquaintance and yells, "Hey there!" as if we're friends. The terrifying arm of the machine is turned on and the man yells, "Brother, give us a smile, I'm taking your picture!" And I try to smile at the camera as Sarah my mother always asked me to do when she took me once a year to Nachlat Binyamin Street to have my picture taken against a jungle background, or next to the famous vase in a studio near Mughrabi Street with goldfish that didn't really look gold in the black-and-white photos but that everybody knew were goldfish. I ask the pudgy doctor about the children in the carts at the entrance, and the doctor looks pressured and says, "What children, where?" I say, "What do you mean where? At the entrance," and he strokes my forehead and says, "Don't worry," but once again he doesn't have a pen that writes. Once again they find a pen. Once again I sign and once again frost. Doctors and nurses gather above me around a darkening flower that is honored and opens and the words rising in my brain are: light of glory. There is no time in me. And the light is glory to the blinded dull eyes. I want to tell the nurses Ada and Tsilla that my ears are dulled to the voice of women; I'm curious but also tired, I'm hovering with fatigue and now have to honor the searing cold that is cutting me. Groggily, human beings are seen lying or laid in numerous cubicles, waiting for operations, then suddenly Nakhtsia Hayman sits up in one of them, waves to me, and even manages to smile, that sweetie. Each of us is closed in his cubicle, the butchers in their green scrubs attack me and I'm not armed and the slaughter begins.

Afterward, they explained to me that the anesthesia was too strong. I saw two people above me smiling, gesturing. I didn't know where I was. I saw voices of nurses and a doctor wearing a dress and singing. I'm amazed but nobody's paying attention to me. I yell, "Get me out, I'm cold!" But nobody responds. The bastards don't hear. A doctor bursts out of the main entrance and hits me with a stick, but that doesn't matter to me because I'm imprisoned in a big block of ice, freezing in it and at the same time leaving our house at 129 Strauss Street corner of Ben Yehuda and it's hot, on Yom Kippur, 1940, the year of "the teeth of the wicked shall break," and I stand with the bicycle in the blazing heat wave, one of those that happened in the world when I was still young, so I stand in line at the ice warehouse at the Dizengoff corner of Arlozorov Street, across from the big sycamore that also died long ago, and I wait to buy a block of ice for the day after the holiday that fell on a Sunday, and I put the whole block in the basket, tie it with a rubber band, and ride home. Around me ride dozens of men wearing undershirts, with blocks of ice in their baskets. The ice drips and melts in the heat and the street fills with water. Suddenly my block of ice bursts and falls and I drown in the cold water and feel dread, but I'm frozen again in the enormous hall, frustrated, I yell and nobody hears. I don't grasp how they don't hear me. And in middle of what I know is absolute foolishness I try to burst out of the block of ice, choking from the stench, but I can't, want to understand who are the deaf people around me, what is the nurse saying who's standing so close to me, what is she whispering in the ear of the doctor who's now exchanged the dress for an army uniform, and I see the white gloves on her hands and her sorrowful white shoes, and then, humiliated and poor, I wake up in bed in the recovery room.

I don't know how much time passed. I was swaddled and I vaguely remembered that I was operated on, but not exactly where. I remembered the ice I was in, my sweet daughter Naomi lied and told me I looked good. I said I had frozen and they didn't notice. For two days I rested. They brought a nurse to stay with me at night. She was so ugly that even in my condition, I decided to pretend I was sleeping. She looked at me with resentment mixed with relief, she fell asleep and snored a little for the hundred shekels she cost, and I thought about the Polish officer who went to a woman he found in the Atom Bar on Ben Yehuda Street who said, "Five liras," and he said, "A Polish officer doesn't take money." Two days later, I walked with Naomi and Miranda to a candy counter in the lobby to drink coffee. After I drank I went back to bed and started getting better.

Next to me, in the room where I was transferred, lay a rabbi who prayed all the time but who also laughed. Until then, I hadn't known any laughing rabbis. I asked him where I could find out where they took my cancer. The rabbi, like all those who hear the word "cancer," looked a little scared and muttered that in general the cancer is cut out and a small part of it is kept in the hospital laboratory and the rest is buried in what he called a grave garden. "Where?" I asked the rabbi and he said, "If it's from a Jew, then with the Jews. But there's no obligation in the Torah to bury a body part of the living, according to the commandment 'but thou shalt in any wise bury him that day,' which was said only about a dead person, but even though there's no obligation to bury, there's no negative or positive ban." He added that authorities on the former set a rule, although not a religious law, that a living body part is to be buried not because of the commandment "but thou shalt in any wise bury him that day," but so as not to trip up the priests, because a priest is also defiled by a body part that isn't a whole dead man. The rabbi cleared his throat a little and looked at me in amazement and added, "Listen, wait a day." He said and I waited.

A friend came to him, also a rabbi apparently. They prayed together, and then he told me that he had found out from the friend, who found out from the Burial Society, that my cancer was buried in Kiryat Shaul Cemetery, Section B, last row. He gave me the number of the grave, which isn't yet covered with a tombstone, and added that the Burial Society accepted the body of a Jew named Jack Konick, a poor cantor from Newark, New Jersey, who immigrated to the Land of Israel to die there and came to park himself here until our holy Messiah comes, but he didn't have enough money to be buried in Jerusalem, and my cancer was buried with the body of Jack Konick, the cantor from New Jersey, in Kiryat Shaul, and unlike the arid graveyard called the Yarkon Cemetery, which looks like a concentration camp for the dead, and only a few people are happy to be buried

38

there, Kiryat Shaul isn't a bad place to be dead in, if you're a Jew of course.

I asked him if there wasn't some Law of Return for cancers that aren't Jews that were borne honorably by ants who seemed to love them very much. Could they be buried in a Jewish graveyard? And he said angrily that cancers aren't cancers but growths, and they aren't circumcised but they aren't uncircumcised either. They're a body part of a Jew, and so they don't need a Jewish mother or a proper conversion, and they're not even mentioned in the Torah as nonkosher, and they're buried by the Burial Society, but only when connected to Jews. Maybe that's not exactly what he said and I forgot. When I told him that cancers called crabs are an excellent food, he was offended and said, "Not our cancers." He wanted to console me and I felt so sorry for him because I found out later on that he died before I did, but not like I did; he didn't come back to life even though he certainly prayed a lot more than I did.

And I lie there and miss the cancer that was in me and think, Who dared to put it in the ground? They could have waited until I go. And what kind of burial did they give it? The rabbi, who had had an operation like mine, said, "Listen, there's only one burial." I asked him if they also toss the cancer into the grave like some Jew, because I'll never forget how they tossed the body of Moshe my father into the grave, they don't even toss out a rag like that, and he didn't get mad but looked pained, and said that a cancer isn't buried as a Jew, and isn't buried in a prayer shawl. Then he raised his voice, "And not a rag! What rag? A prayer shawl isn't a rag," and he looked at me and pitied me for that living death. And I made him laugh. So he laughed and said, "The cancer is buried not in dust, for it didn't come from dust, it came from you, and is in a box that says it's from the right side of the body part, as you told me." I asked what difference it made which side it was on, and he told me angrily and ungraciously that it really doesn't matter, "But remember, your Jewish cancer is buried next to Jack Konick, who was a Sephardi Jew, and that's because of the Russians, since most of them aren't Jews, and so the graves of the Ashkenazim have become rare, and there's nothing more awful than being buried next to a non-Jew, even if you're a cancer. Even a Jewish cancer is a Jew."

After that conversation I left the hospital on a very noisy train. Mendele Mocher Sforim was the engineer, but he was also blind. I got to the graveyard. Next to the graves of Moshe my father and Sarah my mother, I saw a small sign with the name of Jack Konick from Newark, New Jersey, even though my parents weren't Sephardim. I stood there, the train went on, a tiny plane passed by in the sky, I came there apparently because I was sad about the cancer, and in a few more days I leave and that's it, no metastases. I considered myself lucky. I wasn't mad at my cancer, because it was me and I was it, by a kind of covenant, but I was mad at cancers in plural. Sons of bitches. In the ward, I saw people demolished by them. People deprived of their human image by them. Breasts cut off. Wretched women weeping silently. Men with cancers that killed their lungs, pancreas, with metastases to the liver, looks of ruin, of sadness, of disgrace. Next to me lay a man who had been given only a few days. I didn't know then that that was what they'd say about me a week later. But to see how all those people who had once been healthy and loved and ate and ran, and didn't even smoke, and took care of themselves, or those who didn't, and suddenly the cancer creeps into them and destroys everything in its path, may the memory be wiped out of the agent of the omnipotent god seen here at the end of life as a messenger, like the one who told Lot that Sodom and Gomorrah would be destroyed, and he doesn't say a word, doesn't interfere, doesn't plead for the lives of thousands of human beings, and that's it, God says, and there are no questions. If that's God, Satan is a lollipop. If that's how it is, the cancer, like Hitler according to the Lubavitcher, is a messenger of the Lord, and so I think, may the name of both of them be wiped out. Amen.

When I come back, the rabbi's gone. Maybe they took him for tests. I feel as if I'm flying with a lightness that fills my head. I'm riding with Sarah my mother on the 5 bus to my Aunt Bluma who lived on Amos Street. The nurse

Marina said later that that often happens when you come out of operations. She said, and I was sorry she thought she had to say this, she said there was no rabbi lying next to me and no train on Weizmann Street, and why all of a sudden were they mourning for a braid? That's because I told Marina that my aunt Bluma mourned furiously for seven days and seven nights for the braid of her beloved daughter, and Moshe my father refused to come to her shiva but she touched my heart and the heart of Sarah my mother with her awful love for her daughter, with her innocent mourning for her daughter's braid. How wonderful it was to sit for seven days of mourning with my aunt sobbing for her daughter's cut-off braid and seeing people coming in, looking grave, in dark suits in the Tel Aviv heat, and whispering together in Yiddish or Polish and kissing my Aunt Bluma and bending over to kiss her daughter Matilda. Afterward, everyone sat in armchairs or on sofas and drank tea and ate Frumin cookies and cursed the evil fellow who cut off Matilda's braid, which had grown for fifteen years. They talked angrily about the lad, who admitted he had done it out of love. They came from the Jewish tears of Tarnopol, and all Jewish chronicles are written in books of tears. So they sat and wept and one woman from Tarnopol even wailed, and I told her, "By the rivers of Babylon," and she said, "Here by the Yarkon, near the slaughterhouse, and that *shegetz* with his love should be put in jail."

Meanwhile, I slept. I was thirsty and got up. Miranda came and went. They took my temperature. They gave me injections. They treated me with liquid they flowed into me. I lay alone several minutes and the private nurse was still there. I lay in a kind of torpor for a day or two, maybe three. After the two operations I was apparently tired and stunned with visions from the injections I got, the sores hurt me where I had been stitched up twice and I tried to understand what was happening; my bad, fragmentary thoughts crept. Miranda brought a newspaper and wanted to read to me, but I rejected her and didn't want to hear. A small flock of doctors walked in unison from one bed to another behind the professor, and none of them looked right or left. At last they came to me, and the professor stopped, so they stopped, too, of course. They didn't look at me, they stood and didn't see, then back and forth they shot medical terms, most of which I didn't understand, and I wanted to tell them that an old patient lay before them, that I've got a name and I also enjoy Latin words, that I always loved those precise words that Moshe my father loved to recite like Horace or Seneca, but they don't look at me, they follow the professor like a flock, and even when I say something, they don't listen but write on a chart hanging on the bed and take off.

I eat, peeing becomes a problem, the nurse checks the catheter and says everything's fine, the doctor behind her smiles suddenly and records something on the chart. I'm left alone in the room a few minutes and Miranda stands in the corridor and talks with one of the nurses and suddenly a sharp pain slices me, I feel something grinding in me, I reach a hand to the right side and see a gigantic hole gaping in my stomach, revealing the stitches bursting before my eyes. The deep pit breathes, rises and falls like a bellows, part of my belly is already poured out and I see that the belly is a flower opening in slow motion, flesh and blood, veins gaping, the stomach is rising and falling, my guts are spilling out and bleeding and Miranda sees from outside and storms in, looks at the open and bleeding belly and calls for a nurse. The nurse looks, grabs her head, and calls for a doctor. The doctor calls for the professor. The professor is seen running down the corridor and putting on an apron, male nurses run in and press the stomach and fix it firmly in a belt. The stomach escapes from under the belt and the belt is now black with blood and the orderlies put me on a gurney. The nurse says that that defeat is more than bad luck. "You're ill starred," she says, "and it's bad luck." The sweet doctor, a palm tree passing by us on the way to another operation, asks, "Why couldn't you try to be less original?" I hear somebody saying it's all inconceivable, they never heard of such a thing, there's nothing in the professional literature about bursting the strong thread twice in a row. They say that with that thread you could hang ten people like me in the air and the thread wouldn't tear, because that's a German thread, the strongest there is, and the Germans know how to make strong and basic things and the chance that that would happen once is zero, not to mention twice, and they say that I'll go into *The Guinness Book of World Records*. I don't give a rat's ass about *Guinness*. I'm exposed, burst, open, and ugly. The sadness disappears, it wasn't enough to accompany me all that long way; the belly didn't kill anyone, I'm in a book of records, a burst body, disasters happen to them every day. For me disaster happens once, and they'll learn what really happened professionally and they'll know in the future even if I die, and because of that, maybe somebody else will have to die afterward, for good or bad, and I'm now on the gurney and taken back to the hell of the giant slaughter.

I don't remember the beginning of the third and last operation within ten days. Everything was done fast. They gave me an injection of something even before I entered the cell. They took my picture. They pulled out the plywood. I didn't feel a thing. That operation stayed in me as if I wasn't in it and it wasn't in me. The red and black flesh I saw some time later I had also seen before. Afterward, when I woke up two or three weeks later from a coma I had sunk into after the operation, I wanted to hug myself, turn myself back into a human being, and then I was like a dead man who came out of his mother's womb and half his flesh is

45

eaten away, because the flesh turned soft and disgusting and a thin and angry smoke rose from it. The body and its open insides looked despicable and unnecessary. I held torn and foul hands toward myself and we couldn't touch one another, and as they told me later, the operation itself lasted several hours. They said I collapsed in the middle of the operation and at times the anesthesia wore off and I yelled in pain and they sedated me again and cut again and stitched again.

When I think about that today, now that everything is past and I've passed and come back and I'm a walking dead man, I know I forgot everything. But since then, sometimes at night, I dream about or maybe ponder my wound in Jerusalem in 1948, and a vague dread that moved in me when I almost died recently at Ichilov comes back. And I picture something indefinable, a kind of enormous light-colored balloon, maybe a root of a dead tree, a lopped-off trunk, with thin roots that look like snakes climbing on it from below and a person who is me lying in a gigantic bed in New York. Snow is falling in the window and across from me is the fir tree of Priscilla, Miranda's mother, who is holding a glass of wine and slicing a veal roast and serving me gravy with green mint jelly. The sight is stuck in me. Then I try to teach Priscilla the song "Lord of the World Who Created" and escape from the tree and he chases me and I'm ashamed to be on display in that garden of murder, then I see Sarah my mother, young, her face delicate and beautiful, running. I think she's running to Freund Hospital to give birth to me, but memory is misleading, and I disappeared to myself from all the memories. I felt how I was sinking, I wanted to yell for help but no sound came out of me and I sank into the ditch and came to a deep amazement.

Maybe I don't remember and am only imagining, but I know I wasn't in any real place during those weeks, and it's strange to know, like someone who knows he wasn't, where I disappeared to. In English, it's easier, *I was nowhere*, and that's how those weeks of coma went. They tell me, "Yoram, for three weeks you weren't here." I don't understand how I couldn't locate the moments that weren't in my memory and that I've been looking for to know how it happened that after three weeks of death, and for no good reason, I started coming back. Right after I woke up, I knew I had touched what's called the end. In that translation from English I understand it better, the nothing that was. There are words in the subconscious that allow me to imagine something I have no idea of. Memento mori, remember death, the silent monks used to mutter in Latrun, at the monastery where Moshe my father would take me now and then to sit and talk about Arnaut Daniel with the abbot who studied with him in Heidelberg. Moshe my father loved to admire the monks and of course to buy wine from them, which he didn't intend to drink.

After the operation, my fever soared, I was told, and among the three viruses called virulent viruses, my virus was the worst. A real rascal, only one antibiotic could help, and it penetrated from the belly to the lungs, and they collapsed. Dr. Szold, who was both our family doctor and the head of the ICU in Surgery B, didn't give up. A giant man, Szold. An outstanding doctor. It was Friday night. The one pharmacy that was open didn't have what he was looking for. The hospital pharmacy was closed. Szold yelled at a nurse, they said, to go find the sleeping pharmacist. The nurse woke him up and he came, the poor man, he opened up and found that rare serum, Szold gave me an injection, and two pneumonias were struggling in me at the same time, I couldn't breathe. It was an emergency, all my muscles had to be paralyzed so I couldn't move a muscle and I would remain completely still; the lungs shut down and they had to stuff me with gas, and when I try to recall those days, I can't remember a thing. But I did see... and if I saw, what did I see? Maybe I didn't see? I don't know. I saw transparent rings flying like giant octopi, and there's a vague memory in me of grass growing down, growing inside with petals into a brown bed of earth I held inside me. Maybe it wasn't. I remember that, after the of "Yoram, wake up" said by the doctors who came to check what could be done. Miranda sat and slept next to me. She was so tired in the pupil of my eye. My cousin Rina came, who talks fast to catch the words while they're still in the air, and maybe I only imagined her. She was my childhood friend, at our grandmother's house on Hess Street. She came into my death now apparently, because when she was born—and this is the story they told over and over again in the family—Sonya her mother died. My uncle Alex met Sonya a few days after she came from Russia and fell in love with her. They got married and she immediately got pregnant. Alex was too much in love to ask her about herself, but she did say that her mother died giving birth to her, and she gave birth to Rina and also died in childbirth, and Rina my childhood love returns to me. Maybe the death placed before me brought her and maybe she didn't come at all, and I was glad she came from her settlement in the south to visit me, but I couldn't show any feelings. When we were children and played at my grandmother's house, I'd have to pretend we were strangers, and we'd walk from my grandmother's house (which was later replaced by an apartment behind Bialik House near the stairs) to Tchernikhovski to eat ice cream at Whitman's. We'd walk on either side of the street, her on one sidewalk and me on the other, and here she is at my sickbed for some reason, mischievous, sweet, and bold, who would steal pencils and erasers at Hepzibah on Allenby Street. Violence is also a kind of wooing and as soon as she could she went to a kibbutz in the Galilee, married the first guy she met, and got pregnant. Nine months later, she came to give birth in Tel Aviv. My mother and my uncle, who didn't believe in superstitions, sat in the waiting room at Hadassah Medical Center and were overcome by dread. I remember the dread, how my nonbelieving uncle lay on the ground and bit the rug, but Rina gave birth to a daughter and stayed alive and there was great joy, and my uncle brought a bottle of brandy and everyone drank and Rina went back to the kibbutz in November 1947, and on December 1, the first day of the war, her husband was killed and everyone understood that the danger had passed.

I get out of bed in the hospital and go for a walk, engaged with Rina, as Sarah my mother would say, to see the condition of her mother in the graveyard on Trumpeldor Street. She holds my hand and weeps. Sonya was the only mother she had, and she didn't know a thing about her. So, apparently, she came to me in the hospital, in my doze, to demonstrate a situation I thought had happened to me and remind me to think about Sonya when she sits before me. She left only one faded photo of herself, my mysterious aunt, and as the man from the Negev told me—I don't remember where I know him from—Sonya opened doors for us all in heaven and was a pioneer in upper space for the Jews who'd be there. So she was the embodiment of the fear that there happens and doesn't care about killing me, but has nothing personal against me. I thought the cancer despises life for good and obvious reasons and so isn't concerned with it, and what may be even more correct, it feeds on it. I stood in his way when he passed, and he had to get inside me, as if reducing the population that grows too fast.

In the war, I also shot without seeing who I was shooting at. I killed and I didn't know who, and I never went to look for the families of the people I killed. As if they deserved the suffering, they suffered because I hit the member of their family. I once went to Venice for a conference of writers on Mediterranean culture, I met a Lebanese man originally from Palestine, who was fond of me, and we walked laughing among the fat doves, and I told him that Stendhal wrote that two young girls sat in Piazza San Marco on an enchanting spring day and drank lemonade and looked happy and one said to the other, "What a shame this isn't a sin!" He laughed. Afterward he told me I killed his uncle in the war in Kfar Saris near Jerusalem. I told him I didn't remember much from that battle but in Saris I shot a Davidka and the mortar backfired and maybe he really did have an uncle there, and he said with a bitter laugh that his uncle told him specifically that he saw me in Saris and remembered how I cleaned a rifle after I shot him, and I said it wasn't a rifle, and he suddenly, so sweet, disguised himself as a nice guy and forgave me for his uncle's death. I said if his uncle

53

of his generation and then the next generation and the next generation, and remained lucid in life and wanted to deliver a eulogy but there wasn't anybody left to eulogize. Then I started writing in the newspaper and he ran into me and started asking questions and I saw all the journalists hiding in the doorways.

I'm told that for many days people stood next to what they thought was my corpse and wept. They said the hospital office was teeming with journalists. The nothingness I was sunk in was an abyss, a womb I emerged from into a charred world, and half my flesh was dead and I hated me. I remembered the place where I was born as a filthy abyss. "The end is the riddle, the beginning is the solution," wrote Kabak in *Shlomo Molkho*, and like everybody I came from noplace and even sought my memory as Yeats sought memory ever since the world was created, but I didn't find it. I did find a dark cave. I remember a kind of something. No tunnel. No flickering lights. No all that garbage of "my entire life passed before my eyes," no nothing. Over and over, I heard "Yoram, wake up," and maybe I cried but maybe I didn't. The slumber controlled by the doctors, who didn't want me to remember the torments, and didn't want me to suffer, and now I'm trying to understand what happened after the weeks of coma and remember very well how I really persisted, I fought not to wake up. I hid behind a screen of imagining and I saw the people standing as if they were human body parts. I made out their sparkling tears, but not the weeping. A fog was before my eyes, I recognized the faces of people who stood in a white halo and behind it were also people I couldn't recognize, and all the time, they said to me, "Yoram, wake up, Yoram, wake up."

And I see a male nurse I know is an Arab, I don't know how I know he's an Arab, but I know that his name is Mahmid, and he sits at the table and pastes bus cards into a photo album and concentrates on his work, and I think about who is he and he is apparently ordered to say every ten minutes or so, "Yoram, wake up," and I lie in the strange bed that looks like a coffin and I can't move. The movements in the space around me are like sketches by Goya. Goya's transparent people. I see the features of those standing before me and I myself became like an etching by Goya. I feel more than see Miranda and Naomi or my sister Mira, but they seem to be flying. Happening but not existing. When I see Miranda's hand, I stop seeing her head. Miranda and Naomi are still spirits and maybe, maybe—that's apparently what I thought—maybe they're seeking reality to enter it, but I want to stay where I am, without fetters. They keep me from sleeping the deep and drugged sleep that is somehow bliss. I'm foggy, can't move a limb. Can't talk. And by no means do I want to wake up. Something is happening to me, I'm even glad that they'll soon stop pestering me and let me sleep forever.

Nurses come, are pious, lift me up, saying I'll feel better, and I'm a fool and want to believe them; they steal me from Miranda, who wants me to stay, but they mock her and take me to the top of the Arison Tower with the gigantic soup bowl as a helicopter pad. From there I see my sea, the sea that knew me throughout my childhood, the sea of the maiden Lichtman, may she rest in peace, with hair sprouting because she's out of razor blades. In the distance the children are seen dressed in bathing suits and wrapped in furs, running from the water and shrieking, and at the same time I find myself in another sea altogether, in the open sea of Herzliya—if God had money He'd live there—and with me is Naomi my daughter. The two of us laugh at the sight of three young girls in bathing suits sparkling with cell phones at their ears, talking and talking, and I find myself on the roof of the Arison Building at Ichilov Hospital and a big canopy stands there.

They lay me on the concave canopy and I plead with them to take me down from there, but in vain. The canopy is supported on four poles, held by four orderlies, one of them an Ethiopian, and darkness intensifies from him and moves and clears and the cold is searing. The nurses stand at my head without looking at me. I'm naked and nude. Why nude all of a sudden, I think, what exactly is nude? Why a roof of a canopy? I'm feverish and tremble, and ask what is nude, is naked nude, and a Yemenite nurse I knew years ago in Morasha tells me, "Listen, child, you're the nudity of your mother," and she bursts out laughing. The fever intensifies and I'm still hanging on a gigantic thermometer that climbs up and up like the plastic thermometer that was sometimes stuck in my rectum. I yell that I'm cold, that I'm freezing, and that the cold wind is whipping me and I ask why don't they lay me down in a bed, why don't they cover me with a warm down comforter, and why don't they give me pills to bring down the temperature, and one of the nurses explains—but maybe that was afterward, and I'm only attaching the memory to another day—that chills aren't related to hot or cold, that cold water has to be poured on the patient, ice water. Then, as in an ancient ceremony of exorcism, they're pouring pitchers of cold water on me and I'm burning and freezing and a nurse tells me, "When you're having chills we have to flood the body with cold water, only in oldwives' tales do you have to lie under down comforters, drink tea, and sweat."

Above me spreads a black sky that looks like the place where I am but I don't know what it is. I'm not on the roof anymore. I don't know how I got down. I'm not cold anymore. I'm in bed and the people at my bed are still blurred. Now they're sitting in a kind of big round hole and today I don't know why it was of all things round, as if it came through the thick curtain of smoke that was frozen, and they're bending over and moving together in big rhythmic movements that bend them over, and as they sit they sway from side to side in unison, and the frozen smoke shades them, they have no faces and they move, and as Sarah my mother would say, they sway like stalks in the wind. One of them is a woman who looks familiar. How come I really don't know her but I do know that her name is Edith Nahman? The name is stuck in me. Like a nail. I wanted to pull it out. I feel ashamed that she's here. I owe her something. She's angry at me and came especially in honor of my death and probably thinks, What a waste of time, I came to make sure but the bastard isn't dead, he's waiting for me, and he came back and didn't even have a nice funeral. She weeps and sways from side to side, but also winks at me mischievously, and I look at her. "Maybe that's not me?" I ask, "Tell me, Edith, why go back home from funerals? They take us stealthily, one after another, a whole generation, and not a day goes by that one of us doesn't go and die. Why travel all the time from one funeral to another? Why be afraid when one of us dies? Unless it rains or there's a heat wave, maybe we should wait at the entrance to the graveyard, set up a house there for anybody who'd like to stay, with beds, a shower, and a toilet, maybe even a bathtub, windows, a little kitchen, a phone, and a television, and you can sit there and not go back home in cars, in traffic jams, in crowded conditions, on the road, with policemen, with crows."

Why is it so important to me to go back there, from the little or not so little understanding and without the ability to call things by their name but only to know them as a tangible vision? Why is it important to me to understand where I was when I wasn't? I saw the lamp above me, I lay supine, and I was sweating. Somebody in the next cubicle was weeping bitterly. Pleading to live. Miranda wasn't there then and neither were Naomi or Mira, and I saw a nurse bending over a gurney not far from me—apparently it would quickly be put into one of the niches. The light grew stronger. Waves of light came and went and I saw myself from above and from below, the wall in front of me became dry and singed and I heard voices, "Yoram, wake up, Yoram, wake up," and somebody, I didn't see who, gave me an injection, the world was concentrated on the ceiling that faded into a river of light and the wall in front of me blurred. There were moments when I knew where I was, and there were many moments or maybe many hours when I didn't. I felt stupid, I didn't know what was happening. I try to imagine myself, half-awake now, lying like a puffed-up giant sardine; the yelling on the other side of the canvas extinguishes waking sleep in me. I'm awakened and see a laser beam from one of the monitors, glistening in the silvery ring in the ear of one of the nurses sitting at the nurses' station reading a book.

For me, she was Vermeer's *Girl with a Pearl Earring*. Something in the painter's mysterious, magical light that no one has yet deciphered. A kind of glimmer of hope touched me and suddenly somebody said in me, "If there's an earring like that, maybe there's a reason to live after everything I've been through," and the nurse put the book down on the desk a moment and sensed my pleading look and got up, came to me, and gave me a blood transfusion, and at the same time I felt a tickle in my shoulder. I tried to move my head, I heard a rustling, my eyes moved in their sockets until they reached the end of the nose, and beyond it I could see the edge of the face of the most beautiful doctor, Dr. Dayan. She was leaning on my bed and maybe even smiled when our eyes met, but she went on working very intently and sawed a kind of earring with the knife she was cutting me with, it seemed to me. I saw the knife in the thin glistening light of one of the monitors. I saw a beautiful woman, wise in her craft, murdering me, and it all seemed as if somebody was telling that to me, and I felt nice. Go know. She poked another hole in me to give me more oxygen, and I saw, or perhaps felt, that she was drawing a ring in the hole in my shoulder, and wasn't that a dimple for champagne, a dimple that bold women at the Algonquin Hotel in New York would drip a little champagne into so an excited man would dare lick it. No champagne here. Only a torn and bleeding dimple wrapped in the smell of a rotting body.

*

61

I sense something positive, almost optimistic in death, that it is the tarrying Messiah. Apparently I should have died as soon as possible so as not to breathe the air that will reach my grandchildren, and I always have dogs and I don't have grandchildren and I can't create grandchildren by myself. Doesn't cancer exist universally? They tell me, "Yoram, you were dead." But that's not what I was up until then. Life after all is subjective; only death is objective. The cancer felt good and comfortable being in me. It established settlements in me, for if God created, He saw long ago what was unjust and he surely said, "never again." If so many hadn't believed in Him, they would have tossed the bodies straight into the sea without funerals, without burial, without stealing from the state areas of land full of bones, and death wouldn't be considered a disaster but a breathing need for nature. Stupid to waste good land on dead people who will crumble and be eaten by ants that will later get fat and hold processions on Zlatopolski Street to take the miracle of death to somebody who will have cancer. God, if He exists, and I get this straight from the horse's mouth, wouldn't have created Himself.

In those weeks when I wasn't in your world, Miranda heard from the doctors that I was a lost cause, but she didn't believe and didn't not believe. She didn't let me go. Afterward, my friend Jay said that not only did I have one leg outside, or two legs outside, but all of me outside, and only Lazarus would have come back. Jay stood facing me during the coma, the monitors proved to him the scientific fact of my death, and he knew that was it and he wept, that man who sees people dying every day. He understood that he would never see me alive again and told Naomi that now only prayers could help me. Today, the doctors also say that it was Miranda who saved me, and I wanted to ask her, "Why did you save me, beautiful woman?" But Miranda wasn't interested and isn't interested in the metaphysical question of whether she believes in her God. Her faith is a religious faith in a deep sense. She didn't go anyplace and ate only what was put in her mouth. She didn't think whether I would live or die, she saw me connected to a respirator and tubes and IVs, and she had to stop me from going. The legends in the hospital say her eyes were beautiful and red. They say her tears were like a colorful halo, thin and delicate. They said she persisted. They said she didn't weep aloud. That they had never seen such an angel. They said they had never see such a lady as a handmaid of life. I know her quiet weeping. After forty-six years with me she could have known that my leaving the world wasn't such a great loss.

Ultimately, in medical statistics, I was a kind of success story because I belonged to the small percentage of failures that turned out to be wrong, and it was the excellent surgeon who told me a long time afterward that it wasn't he who had saved me but Miranda. He added that I myself also fought, but who is the I he says fought? I went through death and

his cubicle. A woman's weeping was heard, a young woman it seems. A nurse brought somebody and I heard them talking and then everything was silent. It was scary to be all alone with the shrieks of the man who was apparently quite young. On the canvas dividing him and me, a kind of kerosene lamp without glass slipped in the dark. It slowly crept on the lighted cloth and I was scared. The quiet was complete and I couldn't even move a hand to press the call button. I thought the kerosene lamp without glass was a medical instrument. It crept into the silence and I lay facing it, hypnotized. It was a painful secret. It had a quiet force, intense and threatening. It made me feel the death of the man in the next cubicle crawling toward me.

I heard how he, who wasn't he, even when he was surrounded by human beings who spoke in a whisper, started dying. It was strange to me that they didn't hear his yells when he was pleading he wanted to live and didn't hear how he cried to God to take me instead of him. They weren't there then. Only I was there. I heard them talking outside next to the door about the food in the hospital they said he didn't eat, that they missed him, and I still didn't take in that I had recently come back from what's called Sheol, and I was the only one in that silent milieu of dead people, and they don't come back, to know where that dying fellow would die. I knew that was in store for him and that it wasn't so awful and I wanted to tell him, "Buddy, you won't feel a thing, shut your eyes, it's just infinity, hug yourself if you still have hands, and smile if you can move your lips, because nothing will help you, sink into pleasant sleep, generous death will caress you and take you gently to the black hole waiting for you as for us all."

The moments at the kerosene lamp and the canvas wall became difficult after the man's guests left. The kerosene lamp moved slowly. Dread grabbed me by the throat, dread not of death but of being caught in an isolation I had never known before. Maybe I was in a panic because I was alone with the kerosene lamp and that was the first time I grasped how alone I was. I waited. I think I was shaking. I remember hearing a song in my mind, "It's not day and not night," and I looked hypnotized and crippled at the blue kerosene lamp stuck above me, and behind it the young fellow was still dying, and I hummed to myself, "Not day and not night, not beautiful and not ugly, not God but an angel falls into the soul," and a few hours passed. Or that's what I imagine. I'm sure the time passed because the kerosene lamp changed color when the light changed, but nothing really changed. I must have fallen asleep, after a while I woke up, the ICU was bright now and a thin light from outside penetrated our niches. The kerosene lamp was still hanging in front of me. It was dimmed and looked different in the meager light from the windows. And then the kerosene lamp began slowly creeping up. It was somber and shrouded in gloom.

It moved nonstop and now became yellow, and maybe really did look like a yellow spot, that is a yellow star, and moved, and I thought it despised me. Today I think I felt it was talking to me. And then it came to the head of the cubicle and seemed to fall on the other side and disappeared, and just then a nurse came and started taking care of me. She asked why I was shaking, I tried to explain but I couldn't talk.

A day passed. Naomi came, splendidly beautiful, and she looked sad and pensive and serious, and I thought of the nameless man behind the curtain. It was important for me to know that a certain defined somebody was lying there, not just a magician of a mysterious kerosene lamp, who wasn't just a person, not just some "person," but somebody who had a name and wanted my death for his life, and so I had to know who he was. In fact he was also an enemy, didn't I hear him persecute me with his prayers and ask his God to take my life instead of his, and he didn't know that it didn't matter to me anymore—what, one more death, one less death, what difference did it make, even if he was dead now, even if his body was taken away while I was sleeping, even if the kerosene lamp came to clear it out or to harm its shadow, or to touch its echo. And then I thought that what was proper was that the rabbi who sent me to Kiryat Shaul to seek my cancer's grave, the one who could laugh, would come instead of the stupid rabbi here who passes by me now and then but is afraid of me, afraid to see me and to see death because I came back from the place he prayed against. He's with the hospital, and helps those who don't come back and kisses mezuzahs and soils his ritual fringes in soup he carries in a plastic cup in his shaking hands, and drinks the cold soup yawning and slurping, and walks around here with nothing to do and eats free bread and gets fatter from one hour to the next, while the man who really needed encouragement lay here alone beyond the canvas and had no rabbi or even a quarter of a rabbi to help him kill me so he himself would survive.

And I hallucinate Sarah Aaronsohn, how she suddenly got to my cubicle I don't know. Once I knew a lot about her and researched her life and the lives of her friends and I even remembered in the feverish delirium that shrouded me that when she was tortured by the Turks she shouted at her father, who was also being tortured, "Shut up, you're old, you've lived enough." I assume, if I can assume, that my neighbor didn't mean me personally. And yet, I said to myself at the moment, as if to be heard, that I was willing to die, if that would give him peace. Meanwhile, I saw the giant orderlies pushing a gurney into the niche of the fellow who apparently, I knew but forgot, was already dead. Silence. The nurse taking care of me pushed some strands of hair off my forehead and went off. Another nurse passed by my bed and went behind the curtain and a few minutes later I saw the orderlies come out of there with the gurney, which was empty before but now had the poor man lying on it, I was sure.

I found the glow of the beautiful Russian nurse's earring and I saw that she opened her book and the earring still glimmered before me, and as she, or somebody else, cleaned my face, I felt the dead fellow's tears dripping on my cheeks. Before I fell asleep I thought with all my might about that fellow, and I was offended to see how much a human being wants to live. My soul connected with him. I recalled that at a certain moment, facing what I thought was the kerosene lamp without glass, I acted, in my mind, as if I put my hands on my belly near the naval, then in my imagination I pressed a button that looked like a bike bell, and I pressed the button as if it was what separated me and my end. One press of the button. A deep awareness was born in me, out of the smoke filling my head, that I could get out of the world whenever I wanted and however I wanted. There would be no more surprises, my razor blades wouldn't mock me, doctors wouldn't mess around in my guts.

I don't know how much time passed. In the morning, the male nurse on duty came and shoved a thermometer in my mouth, checked the monitors, checked my blood pressure. If I moved a millimeter, the respirator shrieked. The nurse checked the clip on my finger, the hated clip showed the oxygen level in the blood. I hadn't known blood had a dose of oxygen. I'm still inundated with memories of the anonymous neighbor, it's an orderly memory like the stairs of his tormented shouts, and I'm amazed at the beauty of the nurse's earring, and I grasped that there was something, today I don't know exactly what, but a certain joy entered me for the first time after all that unmeasured time. Joy that I could participate in a game, that the emptiness I feel has a name, and I thought, My eyes are staring at the earring that has happiness, if there's an earring, there's hope.

The sad and lonely time flowed. Orderlies I hadn't seen before brought a new gurney to the cubicle next to me filled with a new woman to put in the bed of the dead fellow. Above the canvas separating her cell from mine, a kerosene lamp without a glass crept again, and because of the bright lights roaming and bursting from the monitors, it tried to threaten me, but couldn't. The respirator hummed and cackled like a goose whenever I moved, and the new woman who replaced the dead fellow suddenly shouted, too, and after a while, a day, maybe a week, I think she also died, but maybe she'll die only tomorrow and maybe a few days later. In that factory of death, a cunning silence rules. Funny to see something so banal and to know, as in a cheap existential novella, how close life is to death, how disappointed and superfluous all serious stupidity is. One minute you're alive and one minute you're dead, and maybe the dead woman was taken out of the cubicle after I fell asleep and now maybe it's empty there, but for some reason, I'm sure her body is still here, maybe she's lying dead on the gurney and maybe there's nobody with her, and if she is dead, she's now waiting for the orderlies to take her. The orderlies are the hardest thing to get in the hospital. Nurses come. Doctors. Orderlies—the Messiah comes faster than they do and it's they who take us out and bring us in.

Nurse Darya, who's fond of me, came to make me a sacking in the opening in the chest and she gaped it wide, removed the covering, and told me I'm great but I have to escape through the window—that's what she said, and maybe in Russian it sounds better. Darya said I was hallucinating and it's the strong drugs they're filling me with, hallucination isn't like a dream, it's a definite but incorrect reality, and she'd go on for some time so I wouldn't be scared.

Thoughts were very slow and at a low dose. Even the words in my brain moved slowly. It took me time to find a certain word in my brain and to check it. Passive and alone, I'd watch the drama put on by those who came to see me. Today it's hard to know how long the coma lasted and when the recovery began. Sarah my mother would certainly have said, "There are many sides to everything," and I'm told that one man came to pray for me and they didn't know who he was, and somebody else said it was Elijah the Prophet and I thought, not that serial killer, just not him, not someone who invented murder in the name of God. Maybe that was a hallucination.

I look straight ahead. See a transparent screen. On the other side of the screen blinds are hung and behind them tears are hung, and then people seem to be standing around the tears. I was calm and angry and a spirit of quiet stubbornness lay in me and I fell asleep again a little, or not, go know, and I felt sorry for the talented little girl I suddenly sat with—she looked like a mincemeat of person, cut up and put into five shoe boxes on the wall of the house of a Christian couple I'm visiting now in Beirut, because there's a war in Lebanon and the Israelis are blowing up Muslims. They tell me the girl was buried cut up in five shoeboxes and the gigantic photo of the boxes is hung not just in their house but in their bedroom and they're handsome and polished and wear fine white clothes and they've got a private army and a Mercedes next to the house and a French servant, and the daughter was murdered and cut up by the Palestinians in Tel al-Zaatar, and all night long they look at her, those professors, in bed, in a room barren of pictures except for the photo of their dissected daughter in the shoeboxes. Then I sensed that right next to me, in the cell of the poor fellow who died and the woman who may be dead now, too, they had now brought somebody else. But maybe they moved him, too. I was deader than they were and now they're more dead than I am. I heard noises from there. One man said the cubicle was too small. A woman asked somebody if her husband could drink. They talked about operations.

I hear a woman weeping and I see the back of a familiar nurse bending over and stretching over the woman. I hear her talking as she gives her an injection. I hear her say, "I'm sorry, but this is going to hurt you." I'm tired and the time that passed was ultimately only a few minutes. The dread has become thick and gloomy. At the nurse's station, a short nurse sits down, puts narrow glasses on her nose, and quietly reads a newspaper. I don't ring for her. She looks over at me and can't see me because of the lights. I notice the giant gas balloon leaning on the wall next to me, waiting for when I'll need oxygen again, it's painted silver and red.

I was too alive to be indifferent. I had sweet moments of dread, but also some of the hardest I ever had, because I'm talking only about disappointed solitude, which is hated solitude. I was angry about something but I don't remember what. I saw myself sitting in a chair. They were shooting at me. I didn't move. I said, "Shoot again, what, didn't they teach you to aim?" And the button to call the male or female nurse slipped from its place and was hanging on a thread next to the bed. I felt bad. I knew I wasn't shot, but I wasn't sure. I tried to make noise, but I didn't have any way to do it. Nobody saw or heard me. I had no contact with anybody. After many attempts and great toil, I managed to move an empty cup on the nightstand, but it didn't fall or make a sound, and I almost managed to touch the side of the bed, I tried to push the nightstand with what strength I had to make the book on it drop and make noise, but I couldn't. One of the nurses forgot to leave the curtain open, and so I lay hidden somewhat from the center of the ICU. I wanted to know what time it was, but the clock was on the little nightstand and they forgot to put it close to me and I couldn't see the location of the hands. Everything looked blurred in that space, and from the small windows torn in the wall, pleasant monotonous wails were heard. I felt I was outside who I was, swept up and I don't know where, and there was in me an angry sadness bigger than I was and harder than any dread I ever had.

I didn't think what I was feeling because I wasn't able to think, and I felt betrayed because of the yellow patch I thought was a kerosene lamp without a glass cover, and there was a smell of death and noise from the cubicle of the fellow who died and from the body of the woman who replaced him and died and because of the other one who was brought there and the death that came after him, and voices were heard, I couldn't see them, nobody saw me, the light above me wasn't turned on.

People were lit up in the distance. I saw about ten backs of orderlies or scientists sitting with faces turned to the big monitors and for a long time I watched the people who looked like monkeys through the curtains. Some of the people closest to me were among them, but I didn't take part in the performance they were putting on. Male nurses, female nurses, nursemaids, orderlies, doctors, a woman, a daughter, a sister, friends—I looked at them and didn't always see them. When you're fainting and awake, you withdraw inside and hurt all by yourself. My pride of life rose now above the self-disgust I had drowned in all my life. Many times I knew a smile rested on my face and everybody saw it on me and thought it was me but I was still cut off. Don't hear. They thought I was smiling at them. Maybe I wanted to remain incognito and the smile was a mask, and not deliberate, against my will. People here agonized aloud about whether I recognized them or understood them and I didn't always know who the people talking were and sometimes I did know but couldn't place them and sometimes the hallucinations interested me more than seeing people, even loved ones. Suddenly I understood that there's something positive in watching spectators. I think the moment when I really returned to the world was when I started feeling and sensing Miranda, who burst out of the darkness and looked real, a woman, my wife, in the clefts of my deep recognition and not a dream, not a hallucination, and was or looked so tired, and I wasn't yet sure I knew where I came from but she did know, even though she wasn't there with me on the other side, because one thing I do know for sure is that there, in the other place, in the dark where I was, in that shit, I was all alone.

I try in my mind to curse all the healthy people here, those who come to bark quietly and shed crocodile tears; their floors high, and they wash thousands of pillowcases in it, tens of thousands of blankets, pajamas, linens, diapers, and all those are cooked every day in a giant tank, and the blankets alone could have covered Bloomfield Stadium, and I hear, all night long I hear the giant bellows rising and falling; maybe it's not a bellows, maybe I'm only imagining it, maybe the noises are the groans and weeping and wailing of all the patients, brothers in their isolation facing the nice life going on aloud around them as they shout in a whisper, and from one corner of the universe all that silence shouts, the sobbing, the weeping, the death, and the sadness, and only patients like me can hear it and not the young nurses and not the visitors and not even the girl in the short dress leaning over somebody at the end of the room. Today I have no idea what that really was, I wanted to ask and didn't, because I had no voice and also because the thought of an enormous tank, five stories high, boiling and crushing and clasping and pressing all our pajamas, stirs amazement in me and envy and I don't know who I envy.

I woke up at the visit of the nurse on duty with the sound of the giant bellows inside me. The bellows that played for me night after night. And there were also IVs, some nights they stuck needles in my hands, they connected them, there were treatments, procedures, and all the time they filled food and drink and drugs in bags hanging above me, and they changed the dressing, the most despicable blow. You lie, they open one of the breathing openings they cut in your chest, put in tubes, and pump. Every single nurse who did that apologized, they knew how much it hurt and felt sorry for me, but they said they had to, they had to clean out the phlegm because of the respirator. One day I swallowed a small sliver that broke off from the feeding tube and it spun around in my throat and hurt. I tried to spit and couldn't, I tried to swallow and couldn't, and it hurt me and scratched my chest and suddenly I could talk. It did come from the stomach, and I did have to move one of the valves set in my chest, and I did sound as if I was talking from a very deep pit, but it was nice to talk. Apparently I laughed, and maybe that's what I remember today, hearing my thick, coarse voice. Just then it was the time for the doctors' rounds, and they looked haughty and larger than life and they followed the professor like a flock of crows dashing after the Lord of Hosts. One of the male nurses tried to get the splinter out of my throat, but one of the doctors stopped him to examine me. It was incredibly irritating. I shut my eyes. The professor asked what had happened. The nurse was quite scared and told him. He was waiting for the doctors to leave. But the professor stopped and bent over me, looked deep into my mouth, and I cackled and saw that his eyes were burning, suddenly that gigantic man looked like an excited boy. He asked them to wait for him, apparently he didn't want anybody to move. He skipped to the corridor like a youth, and all of them waited for him without moving and nobody spoke. The male nurse wanted to come close to me but the resident doctors didn't let him. God returned carrying something in his hand. He said, "Now I'll show you how to put in a feeding tube."

He sat down on the bed and I felt him shaking with excitement. A sharp smile crept onto his face. King of the ward, flower of the nation, god of the hospital, he shook and prepared as if in just a little while he would swim across the ocean. His doctors, in blue scrubs, lined up around him in a semicircle, and one of them, I don't remember who, said excitedly, "Now you'll see how that's done!" as if Houdini had dropped in for a visit. Their eyes sparkled. They crowded around, and between them the nurse's eyes were seen and maybe even those of another nurse, maybe the nurse Alex, whom I loved, and two female nurses, too. All of them stood there shaking with excitement. The professor smiled. His smile was worth gold and I add the words "worth gold" now, then I didn't think about gold or worth. His body drew in and his precious hands didn't shake. He brought them to my mouth and cleaned the throat, and then pulled a clean sliver out of the packet he had brought before, examined it, removed a transparent paper wrapping it, and all at once, with a sharp blow, he stuck it with his own hands straight into the depths of my throat, precisely, like a magician, and shot the sliver inside. I writhed in pain, but it was brief, and he raised his hands and one of the doctors grabbed one of them and the show was over. He stood up, stretched, smiled, adjusted his lab coat, and didn't even look at me. He went off, a triumphant smile on his face, the crew of doctors marched behind him in total silence.

Time passed. A month after I came back, one of the doctors came and said they were transferring me to a nearby isolation room that was part of the ICU because I had to be isolated because of the predatory virus that was still in me and a place had been cleared for me there. Orderlies came and moved me to the isolation room, which was quite big. I was alone in it, there was a fear of infection. As the home of a fatal virus, I said to myself, I'm something. I don't think I felt the virus, but I did think about it and consoled myself with the knowledge that it was still dwelling in me. They told me that a skull-and-bones symbol was hung at the entrance to the room, and red and white banners were spread to keep people out. The room was long, with a window near the bed where they put me. All I saw in the months that followed was what was reflected in that window.

There was a place there for another patient, but they said few people were brought here and if they were, they would erect a partition. Only one person was brought and he stayed a few days. There was also a fear of infection from his violent virus, even though it wasn't the same family as my virus; you had to know the difference, maybe one was female and the other male and maybe they would fall in love with each other and leave me alone, maybe they'd even name me godfather to their offspring, and suddenly I felt a profound anger. Why am I driving myself crazy and what am I seeing before my closed eyes? Sarah my mother comes and wants to feed me porridge. I talk to her about my bones. And suddenly she moves but is still sitting near me and trying to make me drink milk, and in fact maybe I do have a fever. I talk with her about how I'll look in the grave. How the ants will eat me. Will my mouth be gaping and my eyes wide open in the ground? The Christians are lucky, their eyes are closed before they're buried, and maybe I won't get lucky and won't manage to convince Miranda that I don't want a grave and that I want to be cremated, and now there's a company in Israel called "Fallen Leaves" that cremates Israeli Jews and non-Jews, too, and it costs only nine thousand shekels, not including the urn, and if I can't be cremated, what will I do? I'll lie and wait for my flesh to fall off. The ants' meal is faster among the Jews than among the Christians, because in Israel they don't bury you in a coffin, and my flesh will be gobbled up quickly, I'll be a kind of long and luscious meal for millions of creatures that will devour me until my bones gleam white.

I talk to Sarah my mother, who is today herself white bones in her grave, but I see her sitting next to me, I annoy her with that talk, I remember she always warned me that

And then the other person was brought to my big, ugly isolation room. Orderlies brought him and erected a partition between us and I couldn't see him. I don't remember where I was, only the sweet and cruel smell of Sarah my mother, who dared give birth to me from the black hole and only when I came to its end did I understand, or I think I understood, what a disaster it is. The man next to me was very sick. Between hallucinations I heard he was a doctor and also a rabbi and an American, and dreading and suffering the pains of hell. When they brought him into the room he was shrieking in pain. Never had I heard such shouts, he sounded like a slaughtered animal, like the cows I heard shrieking and pleading at the old slaughterhouse on the street with a name I've forgotten near the Yarkon River, near my grandfather's house on Amos Street, and whenever a nurse touched my neighbor to treat him he would shriek even more. Most of the time he didn't know where he was. His wife was short, plump, round, and full of love for the air around her husband, and she talked with him in English. She sat with her back to me, but the partition separated halfway and I could see half of her, with her back to me, sitting carefully so as not to disturb her husband's air, wearing a wig that didn't sit well on her hair and talking with him and reading him stupid illustrated Hasidic books for children.

Sometimes his sons also came. They would talk with him without knowing if he heard. From what they said, I then it's dark, and like acrobats they climb to the sky on the sunbeam.

Big fat pigeons danced on my windowsill and the poor wretch couldn't share the pigeons with me. His wife said I was lucky the pigeons were dancing for me. "For my husband," she said, "if they saw him, they would probably sing." I said that a Jew was walking in the street in Minsk and a bird crapped on his head and he raised his head to the bird and said, "Ah, and for goyim you sing!" And because of her poor husband she tried not to laugh. The pigeons' window was hidden by shutters and horizontal Venetian blinds that distorted the distances. The close by looked far away and the far away looked close by. It took me a long time to figure out what side of the hospital I was on. Once the pigeons didn't come and I missed them and once I heard the voice of Ralph Klein from the next room. There was some basketball game, friends had apparently come to him, they roared at every basket, got mad at every missed basket, and analyzed the game at the top of their voices, and I thought, Who said there's no life in the rooms of death?

But I felt close to the enemy and I heard old people waiting in line, I don't remember where, they said they were waiting to get to the next world, and I thought, if indeed I did think, or if somebody really spoke, I heard somebody say, "What exactly is the next world? What exactly does it mean that he went to his world? What world? What went? Why are we afraid to talk plainly? What is this rubbish?" And out of a deep slumber, I heard somebody with a familiar voice ask Miranda, "What, Yoram passed away?" And I wanted to say, "What passed away? Who passed away? You don't pass away, you die." What is it you call the world of truth? Why is the graveyard a house of eternity?"

A few hours passed. Maybe. It was sad in the web of uncertainty spun in me. And I rebelled, lying free and hanging in the air above the bed. I knew I wasn't dreaming, and I wanted to go up and up and Naomi disappeared for a short while but Miranda remained. Then she also left. I'm alone and people come from the days when I worked on a ship, fat Menahem, Zaki, Zucker, they take me to Lish and to Abou Lish and Lish's dog jumps up to hug me, he's not Topsy who bit me, and I'm alive and next to me is Lish, whose brother Shemesh was with me in the platoon and took gold in Katamon and bought himself a house in Yad Eliyahu and put up a high antenna for the radio and climbed on it and fell and died, and Abou Lish tells Lish to bring him some cottage cheese from the store, and the dog jumps, brings down the storekeeper, grabs the cottage cheese, and brings it to Lish and then they sit with me in a small hotel in Haifa, in the same room. There were twenty of us sailors and a curfew was imposed. They distribute IDs because the Yishuv decided to be a state. We wait. The nerves of the sailors with me melt in the heat and fat Menahem brings a toilet from the hut because he felt like doing something and two whores come from Naples and I run away and they chase me and put me into a fax machine, a black and modern machine and somebody there, I don't know who, hits me and stuns me until I take on the shape of a shroud and he puts me into the fax, I hear the dial tone, which is different from the fax tone, and I'm drawn in. I'm sent far away from here and feel light, I like being a fax sent to a place far from the hospital. I feel on my body the words written on me, reach the window, the rustle of the sea, the hostility of no gutters, the hostility of death I now recall, and that says something about today when I'm still alive and how was I sent as a fax to noplace and at the same time I'm here with nurse Julia, who's now smearing a green salve on my behind.

I'm a man of seams, and nurse Julia is wearing an earring, and maybe also a ring, and she's got such a Jewish face, and she's lean, soft, and something turns sour in me, I didn't give her anything, I owe her, but what? Maybe the giant viruses climbing on the walls of my body and looking like rats. I see the rats lying in wait for the weak patients washed by young women who talk about handsome young men who are swaying like peacocks and singing perverse songs and talking nonstop on cell phones and are wonderful and dreadful and young, and in my mind a Hasidic song is humming and also humming quietly is Alterman's song about the moon and the cypress and can you still ask their who he is, maybe it's Morom Morom, whom I made up and wrote about in a book that was never published, and he probably says "desire" instead of "want," something that caught the spiritual and bohemian naïveté of the 1920s. The man's hair is silvery and a little wild, in a cultivated way, and he's wearing a greenish, old-fashioned corduroy jacket, and a wide-brimmed hat. In front of the man whose face I don't see, and up to the end of the long room, thousands of Hebrew books are on shelves in a splendid disorder, and beneath them, on the shelf facing the man, stands an old radio, an Orion radio that once was, that Moshe my father bought, and it was brown, and made of mahogany, and it was a radio with eight tubes, and from this radio bursts a fiery speech by Shmaryahu Levin that changes to a belligerent and dramatic speech by Zalman Shneur, and Shneur's bold speech changes back to Shmaryahu Levin's fiery speech about the painful fate of the Jewish people. And the man whose back is to me starts weeping. He takes off his hat and pulls out his hair and spreads his arms and starts bleating: "Where did the Jewish people disappear to? What happened to the Jewish people? Where is that people? How did such a disaster happen? How did they let a people die like that?"

He sobs and doesn't get up off his chair and I feel his real pain, the grief that gnaws at him, and suddenly some noise is heard and a woman runs in, apparently she lives nearby. She wipes the man's forehead and calls him by a nickname, it seems to me she said "Sweetie," such a name, *Sweetie*, Sarah my mother had a friend named Sweetie and she says excitedly, "Sweetie don't aggravate your beautiful eyes don't hurt your wonderful eyelids," and she turns to me and says angrily, "Why did you come here? This was a Jewish area, they all disappeared, that happened when Stalin and Beria killed one another, the people disappeared here. Not far from here, in northern New Jersey, the Jews crossed the Red Sea," and she points to the place where the people stopped, sands surrounded by scorched grass and in the distance clouds sailing and Israeli children cutting down trees near Sharona and bringing the trunks and sticking them in the sand dunes between the old city hall in Bialik Square and Allenby Street, and Winston Churchill comes, the minister of settlements of Great Britain, and all of them crowding to see him up close and there was no time to plant those trees and they were stuck in the warm ground for a few days, and are crushed and fall down, and Dizengoff is beside himself, and Churchill tells him, "Without roots it won't work," and the Jew in the room says, "That's it! Roots. The Jews can't be roots."

He keeps pulling out his hair and the woman wearing a wig explains something to me, the man is still weeping and saying, "Let them carry my small intestine, the putz comes from the Land of Israel, arrogant, and will say it's better in Tel Aviv, that it's a small and funny Hebrew city of Zionists, and I'm an animal that lost a people," and I tell him my people went down to hell and he sees me, his face is still sleepwalking, he gets up and falls down and then suddenly lies on the ground, kisses my feet, and says, "There is dirt on your shoes from the Holy Land and what is left of the Jewish people will be buried there," and he bangs the wooden floor with his fist and shouts, "Get out of here, go to your Ben-Gurion, there's nothing for you here, the Jewish people got one knockout blow, it won't be healed, you're an episode in the chronicles of Grandfather Israel, the blow was too great, the world killed the people, you saw how five million Yiddish-speaking Jews were destroyed, five out of six million Yiddish speakers, a million students, who could have been doctors, Einsteins, Freuds, rabbis, sages, were murdered, and your Land of Israel is a joke and nonsense, you'll kill Arabs and the Arabs will kill you," and then he yells, "Get out of here!"

I want to tell him something. A great love for him lights up in me, but I feel ashamed and he yells for me to get out and that he doesn't need me, and I leave with a head black as coal which looks like an egghead, although an egg that could be black, and I get into the isolated car standing not near his house but in a big empty parking lot. The car talks to me and I have to find the road to the right or left and from the recesses of an abyss I see a mouth peeping out of the dark and a man's voice is saying again, "Yoram, wake up!"

I open one eye, see the Arab nurse Matira, who isn't pasting bus cards in a photo album anymore, and for a long time I haven't been with him, I'm in the isolation room, not the ICU, I'm progressing, the doctors say, so why do I have to go on hallucinating all the time and why do I think of the Angel of the Lord who strikes the camp of Sennacherib and kills 185,000 people and they get up in the morning and they're all dead, not only dead, I laugh in my hell, but they wake up to discover they're dead. Out of a combination of the sharp pain in the stomach and songs of the youth movement that keep going around in my head in a loop, I want to weep. A nurse brings me tears from a woman who lost her husband and I put them into my eyes and weep and she opens the cup and I go into it but in fact she opens the small shutter in my chest, inserts the suction tube, I feel faint and she takes out the tubes and I feel the seams.

In the depths of my brain, a picture was painted. I saw the plump nurse who came to wash me, but she was wearing makeup. Somehow, I knew nurses don't wear makeup on duty. If I could have thought and not just imagined, I would have understood that maybe she was part of the auxiliary force. Sometimes they come, nice and baffled high-school girls, full of enthusiasm and good will, to help. The thin makeup apparently on one of their faces reminded me of the dead people I met in New York. I open my eyes wide. The songs are going around in my brain. Mira is sitting next to me, holding my hand. She fell asleep, the poor woman. I see a corridor. Where does it lead? I turn my face away from the young woman who's trying to find one place where she can give me an injection and I'm riding on the subway where the thought that I'm still dead leads me, and I get out, and grab a quick coffee and go to work in the elegant store of the dead on Madison Avenue. There I paint dead people, and a tall man who works with me dresses them. In a corner the radio of the dead plays songs and in the middle of the song "How Much Is that Doggie in the Window," sung by Eddie Fisher, an angry old woman comes in and says we have to use cheaper materials for the clothes, that they're meant for "one journey," and from Italy comes a new shipment of dyed cardboard shoes for the dead smeared with lacquer and they look just like expensive shoes.

I hear a nurse calling me, but I feel good and I don't want to come to her, I feel good in New York, on Madison Avenue, in the city I loved most in my life, and it was hard for me and good there, and I was healthy, although I was afraid of swallowing and I slept whole nights at the entrance of hospitals and I was sure I'd swallowed a razor blade, I wrote a poem then of how I choked to death, all my life I was choking to death. That's the cancer, I said to a nurse and now I know she wasn't there and came from "New York Hospital," where Aya was born years later, and she was in my real youth, with love, with vengeance, and I came to her older than everybody after the horrors of the war and I was there, I was real, freedom, anarchy, and the nurse wearing makeup disappeared and I'm still painting the dead with the help of a tall cold woman who said she was Greta Garbo's makeup artist. I followed her instructions. When we'd finish dressing the dead person, and after a top hairdresser of the dead did his or her hair, we would put the body in a coffin, which was sometimes very expensive and embellished and sometimes seemed as if it were embellished. Family and friends would come and look at the dead person smiling and painted and looking at them, too, and afterward we would fasten the cover with brass screws and six men would carry the coffin to the best limousine in New York, black and splendid, to start the journey to the graveyard.

I wonder. Not sure I know where I am. Where is the girl who helps. Maybe in national service? I'm the nation they come to serve. Long live the State of Israel that sends girls to help me. And suddenly Adele Cohen comes to visit on Madison Avenue, she lives on Eighth Street and studies Egyptology and says that the Egyptians would send the dead person to eternity in a splendid boat on the Nile. I'm almost awake. I have no desire to leave the house of the dead on Madison Avenue and return to a bed in Ichilov. I see my sister Mira now sitting slightly bent over and trying to read a book, and at the same time I see boats taking ancient Egyptian sailors to the next world and there's a lot of charm in that, a kind of wonderful cruising, very beautiful, and at the end of ends there is no splendor, no nothing, but for an ugly wilting old man like me, when everything around is miserable and dying, a picture of a beautiful and pleasant boat sailing me over the Nile to the world in store for me beyond everything is a mendacious but exhilarating sight.

They tell me I look good, but I know I look like an old shoe. I think that at least my burial will be proper, that they'll bury me on Madison Avenue and will paint me and I'll look nice, and I remember or imagine or wonder or weep as the guests in the funeral home in New York stand around the coffin, once or twice I accompanied them to the graveyard in the Bronx, and the priest would finish the prayer and say, "We return your body to the ground, earth to earth, dust to dust, ashes to ashes. May God bless you and keep you and cause His countenance to shine upon you even if you walk in the valley of the shadow of death you will see light and He will be merciful unto you and will give you mercy and rest." And I remember thinking about that journey. I see a funeral that looks like an ancient religious procession, flamboyant, and the coffin carried like a ship taking gold straight to God. And that's how the dead person begins his journey, dressed and embellished, lying in a gorgeous coffin, and they don't just toss the corpse as in Israel, but respect the body, because just recently it was a human being, and I don't know, I also think of myself, see myself as a corpse and me, smeared salves, put the tube into my chest, adjusted it, one of the nurses works like a Swiss soldier, she's one of the only Israelis still working here. She works precisely, devotedly. Cold-bloodedly. She works like a laughing clock. And she finishes and I lie clean. A male nurse comes in with an IV. A nurse comes to adjust the connection to the respirator. I groan. The machine groans back, a fugue of shit and groans, and Miranda comes back and sits and looks at the machine. She's trying to understand what the machine is saying, but there's nothing to understand.

By now I'm seeing differently. The nets they were become human beings. They're cast out of my hallucinations. I hear their heartbeat. See how they turn into corpses floating to the small Jewish eternity. Without an orchestra. Without beauty. Without splendor. Simply like death in truth, nothing. I hear the doctor who comes to examine me and see Goya's drawing before my eyes. Once again, I connect to my two horrible minutes on Mount Zion when I almost died and was saved by an Englishman in the Arab Legion who shot me to kill me and then saw me and loved what he saw and saved me because he didn't shoot me again. I see a picture and they tell me it's beautiful, that's Goya's execution scene and how can an execution be beautiful? Once I stood before *Guernica*. A liquid young man stood there, an Innie once, today he's probably an old Yuppie, and he started laughing and said, "The picture is so funny." I asked, "What's funny?"

He said, "Not *funny* funny, funny that it's so beautiful, look at the head of the horse or the bull." And suddenly the days of the war came back to me and for the second time in my life I hit somebody. And he ran out stunned. They brought a policeman. The policeman was on my side. They told the former Innie putz to go home, that the issue would be taken care of, and they winked at me. I bought the policeman a drink and he said, "Turn your head around so you won't see me drinking on duty."

In my eyes I see Goya's painting, *The Third of May, 1808*. See the French firing squad executing Spanish defenders of Madrid, and one of them, the swarthy one in the middle, the tallest one, with wild hair—on one of his hands you see the sign of the nail of the Messiah on the Cross—he spreads his arms on an imaginary cross and I see the amazing man and across from him one of the shooters whose rifle really touches the man, all of them executed now, but the man in white is already dead, even though he's still living his last and eternal moment and feels it in his body. The man in white is shedding my blood, somebody comes to wipe the sweat off my face, my right hand is bleeding, the man in the painting will die now, he's a kind of process of death, he's that second in me as then in Jerusalem and now, too, the inarticulate second between something and something, Goya, between life and death and vice versa. I imagine the painting in my mind, Goya comes and I'm with him, and now I am only I and maybe me and far from that belonging, I don't care who's more right, the shooter or the shot, one man at the feet of the man in white, who will die in a few seconds, who died even before, was right and not right because death has no privilege of *was*, *is*, *will be*, that's an axis of time that doesn't exist in the life of death. A light shines on the man, you don't see exactly where it comes from, those seconds in the painting are very hard to paint, it's hard to paint the future continuing from the present, and it can't be catalogued, that firing squad will soon vanish from the world, and their children will die, too, and their grandchildren will die, too, no one will know where they're buried, no one will know what they did or where they did what they did, and yet the figure in the white shirt, the shot man with the flashing eyes, with the defiant and undefeated hands, that man will remain alive at the moment of his death, a second before his heart stops forever, in the painting painted by a genius who grasped the unimaginable magic of the awful moment that connects death to what may come after it, life.

Recently, Miranda brought a small wooden board and a thick black marker and I tried to write what I wanted and couldn't; Naomi wrote the Hebrew alphabet on it and the Latin alphabet and I tried to move a finger, letter after letter, so sometimes, but not always, they understood what I wanted. It's evening. Summer. Outside, the light slowly turns toward the room and away from it. A woman came and goes on stretching me as on the rack of the Inquisition, spread out like skin stretched to dry on the side of the bed; she calls another maid, they drag me up to the edge of the pillow, and I lie on the side and see in the distance something I maybe don't see.

In the window, I see Goya's *The Third of May, 1808* again, it doesn't leave me, now it's a movie and a video on the window with the pigeons and suddenly I feel disgust for somebody who is me, and the poor sweet woman taking care of me now when I'm so ashamed, ashamed at the sight, ashamed at the stink, she wipes my behind and my body, and a nurse comes and they wash and dry me together, and I hate myself, that's how I know I'm really here, that I am in fact still alive, and the respirator shrieks, and I feel the gloved hands touching me. Now somebody is cleaning the sore on my stomach. A doctor comes, one of them, I don't remember who, and another nurse comes, and again the treatment. The pain. The shame.

After a while, maybe a day, maybe a week, I weep on the inside, and two orderlies lift me, they hold me the way a veterinarian holds a cat, they lay me in a tub and go off. Two maids strip me and lay me naked in a tub with all the tubes and IVs in me, and I am like a stinking cake in the tub. Folded and certainly looking like a rat. The strong maids look at me. One of them is a Yemenite, and one isn't. They speak Hebrew, and that's new to me, for Russian is the name of the game here, and they start washing me. I shrivel up and shrink. I'm ashamed lying in the tub and try not to see. They toss me around, they have strong hands, pass me from hand to hand, soap me, scrub me as if I were a floor of cartilage and put their hands in the behind, nose, ears, and between the genitals, they carefully avoid the feeding tube and the air tube and play with me like a ball; I'm turned from side to side, and they go on doing a thorough job, turning me over and instructing me to try to bend right or left, but I can't talk and can't move on my own, one of them shouts to a doctor passing by, "Hey, he doesn't move?" The doctor says, "No, he has no muscles," and she says angrily, "Why didn't they tell us?" and the doctor says, "That's how it is," and goes off. I hear and translate everything to myself in a new language born in me, but the translation may not be precise. When the doctor came and took my hand and cut it with aristocratic expertise and put in an IV, it hurt, and he said he was sorry he hurt me but it sounded to me as if he said, "I'm going to get you home."

In my head I'm constantly hearing a loop of songs. And suddenly that song by Pen, "The road looks so long so close is the moon"—"The Drunk Song," and I'm hanging on the wings of the song, hung on spider webs. The woman, maybe a doctor, comes and examines me, and Moshe my father smiles and says, "Quite right, Yoram," so I know that for now I'm alive, like a giant sausage; and the maids, the

Yemenite and the other one who isn't a Yemenite but isn't Russian or Arab either, Israelis who work, and there are only a few, they play with me and I enjoy the way they work. Enjoy their Israeliness, the lack of personal closeness to the insect in the tub who is me, and their thoroughness. I know there's no way I can describe to somebody what's happening with me here, because until I speak or can speak, if my voice ever comes back to me, there won't be anybody to describe it to and I'll certainly forget it all. I look at them, see them from below, and that shames me, and while being washed in the tub, I think, the viruses walking around freely here must be afraid of those giant maids and the diseases flee from them because they're strong and terrifying, and they clean me but they also talk about the party where one of them, I forgot which, the Yemenite or the one who isn't a Yemenite, spent last evening. She said, "Listen, there was awesome music and a little like darkness and mystery and sexiness, and the one I told you about, like really something, honest to God, and Hedy Gee from Germany made eyes at me and that hunk, like he said he's a lawyer or something, I like really fell for him, and we talked, and he felt, he's got like a really great ass, got fresh a little but was like sweet, I liked him." And then she went on, "But he's also got like some sense, he can talk, then we danced," and suddenly she looked at me with a little dread, "Listen, it seems to me like this Yoram is really hearing."

I really am hearing. I'm curled up in a tub. I felt bad being naked and old in their hands when tight, great asses were spinning around in their heads, and I was silent and they discovered my looks. Suddenly they grasped that they were taking care of someone who was once a human being. For a brief moment they expressed a soupçon of sympathy and one of them looked at me as if I were no longer transparent, as if I had a body, and she said I had wise eyes, I was clever, and she added, "Look, he probably had a great ass once, too." Then the other one stared at me and said, "Go know," wiping me. And very slowly, carefully, as if I were made of especially fragile glass, they put me back in the freshly made bed. When they got up to go, one of them, the Yemenite or the one who wasn't a Yemenite, noticed my book, which had recently been published in France—Miranda had brought it to cheer me up—and on the cover was a photo of me when I was young, and the book was about my young life in New York and America, so the maid looked at the photo and seemed embarrassed and she apparently discovered that I really was a human being, discovered and understood that I was once young, and she said, "Look how handsome he was, look what a waste, look at what life is! How everything passes." She saw me puffed up and clumsy and moving my head in real pain, and she didn't know, she only feared, she didn't really know if I could hear and now and then even understand, and she said, "Ya, what a shame that life's like that."

They left. I was tired, cold flowed in my bones. A kind of isolation. Nobody was with me in those moments and I tried to talk to myself, but I had no voice. No internal voice either. I could hum in my mind the loop of old songs spinning in my mind incessantly, but the silence was beginning to be almost pleasant. People travel to India to be silent. Monks go to monasteries to be silent, and I, without traveling anyplace, I was silent for two and a half months in Ichilov, without Indian food and without spirituality, without the meaning of life, without Saint Augustine, without stupid music, and mainly, without gurus. The deaf conversation with myself was dismal. I wanted to hear myself, not to talk, I would go into a kind of superfluous dullness. I thought this must have been how Beethoven wrote his late quartets and the Ninth Symphony. I always wanted to understand how a deaf man could write such wonderful music. Now, in the silence, I began to understand. The imposed silence was hard but also right for me. When you're silent you don't stop talking with yourself. I tried to understand the melody. In those days, when I wasn't hallucinating, I was seeking logic for the lack of logic in silence, after all, the first thing a child does as soon as he can is make a sound.

While thinking and wondering about the maids who had left, I remained with the photo on the nightstand. I couldn't see it because the stand was a little too far away. I think I felt bad not because I'm not handsome and am worn out and tattered but because I remembered the past when I looked like that and I didn't know I looked like that. Now in my old age, I understand who I was, but it's too late. In a meditation, I saw in my mind a short film that may not have been a hallucination, no, it wasn't, it was reasoned into the hallucination, and I knew that the things really had happened, and it's hard for me to understand that. A young Israeli girl whose name I've forgotten and who looked like a movie star whose name I've also forgotten came to visit in Israel when her mother died, and when her mother's apartment on Zlatopolski Street was emptied, she found the wall with photos of me that her mother had found in some magazine, *Monitin*. Her mother, it turned out, loved to look at photos, apparently also out of hatred, said the girl, because she hated beauty, envied beauty, didn't rely on beauty, wanted to be more beautiful than she was, "even though she was very beautiful," said her daughter from the US, where she had fled from her mother, and said she herself despised beauty, but had fallen in love with the photos and also with her mother's strange love, and we met, I was very old by then, we met at Zigel, the club belonging to Zohara, who traveled to distant islands, and the young woman came there by chance and found me and looked at me and was furious at how I looked and left angrily. Afterward she wrote me vicious letters about how I had killed the handsome man she and her mother had loved and how could I have done that to her. That sat on the end of my nose, I wanted to tell that to the two maids with the tight ass, but they'd already vanished, and if they hadn't, I couldn't have told them, because I had no voice, and I'm not sure that if I had had a voice and I did tell, they would have understood the rage of the woman who spat fire and brimstone at me and was angry I had killed her great love and called me a murderer.

A year after I recovered, I came to visit the hospital. I just wanted to see where I had been, and it turned out that all the time I had been hallucinating. I felt like the monk who didn't know if he dreamed he was a donkey or if he was the donkey who dreamed he was a monk. But I also remembered things that were. That were very much. It's true I didn't always know where one started and the other ended, but I did feel as if in a pool of objective isolation.

It was said of Sarah my mother that she'd know when to die. In the prime of her life, she often asked me to come with her to see her parents buried on two sides of the graveyard on Trumpeldor Street, and they were so far apart because they died so many years apart, and we went to the graveyard. Sarah my mother wanted to see her mother and father and her dead friends. The only ones still among the living were Miram G. and Elisheva. At the edge of the graveyard were the graves of children, gentiles, a Jewish prostitute from

Jaffa who married an Arab, and a lot of solitary people. Sarah my mother would stop at some tombstone and say, as if to herself, in pain and sadness and with her own logic, a sense that deceived her all her life, and with a visible joy that I was also listening, "See, Sarah? You were right. They died and abandoned you." Maybe there was also a tone of vengeance in her voice, and she would stop at the ancient tombstones and say, "Oh, she found Haim in the garden, oh, here's Manya, here's mother, here's Sheinkin, here's Teacher Bograshov, and here's Sheinkin, and you know that Sheinkin was the one who called Tel Aviv Tel Aviv? There was a place in Babylon called Tel Aviv, that's from Ezekiel, and here's Ahad Ha'am..."

Most of the streets of old Tel Aviv are buried there, the graves are abandoned, downtrodden, and the grave of my grandfather, who died in 1917, looks bad and peeling. Sarah my mother wanted to fix it up because she was mad about her father, who betrayed her and died so young. "But you don't fix up the tombstones of grandfathers," she told me, and she smiled at me sadly and compassionately. And on some of the tombstones was one word: "Solitary." A young man got off a ship and who knows where he lived, maybe he was killed in the pogroms of 1937 and maybe he just died. Since he's buried under the sign of "Solitary." He came to the city, and maybe he didn't fight in the pogroms of 1937 but was killed by a stray bullet, maybe he shot himself because he fell in love with the daughter of one of the farmers in Ness Ziona or Petah Tikva, maybe he just came to die in our land and they didn't know who he was and they dug him a grave and what could they write on it? "Solitary." Years later they started writing "Anonymous," but the word "Solitary" was more powerful. The anonymous one is anonymous to others. There are those for whom he is anonymous. A solitary one is solitary to himself. How isolated to be solitary only to yourself. As among the Americans, known only to God. For what can be sadder than a grave placed not only over an emptiness that was once a man or a woman missing a name, but also over someone who doesn't have anyone who knows if there's anybody waiting for him. And I stop with Sarah my mother at Max Nordau's grave. Today young people at his giant tombstone, which looks regal, as if he were the president of the State, ask who was the man who got that giant tombstone. Nothingness reigns. And that's sad, and I think I have no right to be sad, that I want to be a happy dead man.

After the visits to the yard of dry bones on Trumpeldor Street—the most beautiful place in Tel Aviv, a museum for beautiful and bold works of art, with the names of dead poets, with the poems written in the air above the tombstones, and Sarah my mother is right, it's a pleasure to die there, tombstones with wonderful, sad inscriptions, about children who died, about a man who lost a woman he loved, about somebody who was killed by mistake and his wife asks him to ask heaven to forgive her for being alive—Sarah my mother would invite me for a cup of coffee, which she called a glass of coffee, in the Hungarian café on Ben Yehuda Street near Trumpeldor. A waiter dressed like a Hungarian officer, with a bowtie, slightly blackened cuffs, and a suit, a vest, whether it was hot or not, Hungary in Palestine. A small mustache. The man always leaned forward, crooked his arm, held it out delicately with a white handkerchief on his hand, and waited with exemplary courtesy, with a pleasant but impersonal smile, for the order of turkey in silver powder, or filet mignon in mushroom sauce with ground mint.

He looks at us and we order coffee, instant coffee, the Hanukkah miracle of the graveyard, drink the harsh, simple coffee, there is nothing else, and my mother decides to be what she called "bold" and orders some dry cake, too, and we sit in the middle of that Hungary, and on the wall are old Hungarian newspapers in bamboo frames, and a laughing little woman sits and reads a German newspaper. My mother talks about the tombstone for Brenner and his friends, "Twenty-three bodies, we were young in the yard of the gymnasium, and they brought the corpses and put them on the sand, they were mutilated and you couldn't tell them apart, and they covered them with shrouds, then they buried them in a mass grave. And today what? Eighty-four?

How many wars have there been since then? Apparently the same damned war, from the Balfour Declaration to this day and forever and only the battles are different. So look what I've bequeathed you and your daughters, my dear Yoram."


I return to my sickness and all around things are happening and people are changing. Nurses move. Doctors come and go. The cleaning woman looks at me, a small woman with deep wrinkles, even though she's not old, and under the wrinkles is her handsome face; she doesn't understand Hebrew, cleans the room thoroughly and comes to my bed, bends over, carefully cleans around my nightstand, caresses the legs of the bed with a yellow towel, is careful with the cords and strings, and even dusts the giant gas balloon and looks at me affectionately. When you're half-dead you're loved even by the cleaning women who, had they stayed in Russia, would probably have been doctors. I see a spot expanding on the ceiling above me and the spot draws me. The cleaning woman says hello and changes the garbage bag and leaves with the brooms, while the spot seems to say to me, "You're shit," and I ask, "Why am I shit?" and there are so many answers that there is no answer. Then I look at the male nurse who comes in with nourishment and to put in the feeding tube, and I think people don't look at one another here. Everyone seems to be a skein of silkworms and a live butterfly will finally emerge from it. The skeins are indifferent to one another and I'm trampled because I never meant to be sick like that. I thought I'd die from a heart attack or a stroke, and I did have a slight stroke, I know how it feels, while cancer is another story, it's incomprehensible, and without a voice I ask a nurse if he knows why they're keeping us alive, why they persist in curing us. People are groaning and somebody who went through the city and died and was swallowed up in the graveyard on Trumpeldor, if he came back to life today and came out of his grave shouting, real-estate sharks of the dying would swoop down on him, surround him with two-hundred shekel notes because he could get rich just on the money he'd earn from his honored grave's place in that prestigious graveyard where many want to be buried, and his solitariness would overcome the indifference, the fact that in truth no one was looking for him, no one was looking for his family, that's how it is.

One difficult night at dusk, I am terrified and weak and Miranda says she has to go and Naomi can't stay the night. A doctor comes and says they found something good in me. He explains, I don't understand. My friend Jay, who transplants hearts, comes and explains. I don't remember what. Miranda comes and goes again and before she goes she says a word I can't hear and I see, it seems I see, a tear roll down her cheek and I try to understand what cheek it's rolling down. After a while, maybe a day, maybe two days, I suddenly hear from the enormous silence the music from the film *Adam Resurrected* of the Gesher Theater. I guess that, as in years gone by, a circus tent is now set up not far from here, in the museum square. Something connects with the music. Apparently today is Holocaust Memorial Day. Everything is really silent beyond the wall. You can hear the silence outside, and so the music, too, is isolated.

And I dream I am a monk in the desert because it seems I want to say Balzac's sentence that the desert is God without people. And I say it, but no one hears, and I have trouble opening one eye, I remember the trouble well, as if I needed a crane to lift the eyelid. Yes, I remember the weariness that weighs on me and feels good, a small homeland, a kind of statue sculpted in water, and I want to tell somebody about the desire to sleep and about the wearisome rest and a thick blanket of feathers and silence is spread over my face. I cough and one cough starts a long chain of electronic groans from the respirator. One turn on my side noisily lights up lights that rip the background murmur of the monitors. A staff of light gets into my head, I hear the drums, the trumpets, shrieks in silence, and I want to hum those German songs and suddenly I'm not there but with Moshe my father, who lay sick here downstairs even though the building he lay in had been replaced long ago.

I see Moshe my father going down in an elevator. He takes a taxi to Ben Yehuda Street, walks around in the street, and looks for Ernst. He stands next to the restaurant First Cellar, which died long ago, wearing a corduroy shirt with a lot of pockets for tobacco and pipe and flannel pants and an embroidered purple tie, and on his head, as always, is a black beret. I didn't miss him. I didn't understand him. He died thirty years ago without my missing him. When he was young, he played those German songs in the brutal Nazis' clubs, and now I miss him. According to the chronological order of life, my disease, in fact, should have gone to him. Circuits can't be hanging in the air. They have to be closed. I and Moshe my father. In his hand he holds a walking stick he really didn't need. On top of the stick is a lacquered ball, smooth and pleasant to the touch, and his laughing eyes in his bitter and funny sadness. He was a wise man, ostracized by himself, seeking in himself the splendid failure of his beloved William Tell, an erudite man against himself and quite a snob, and as Max the Lunatic said, he was both comic and tragic.

Maybe I am sleeping. But not really sleeping. I see him standing next to me. Here in my prisoner's bed in the isolation room. Moshe my father looks at me with his beautiful, soft eyes, but also with the breaking winter waves, their pleasure is heard in the record of songs spinning nonstop in my mind along with the music of *Adam Resurrected*, and

I would tell all that to Miranda, but she's not here now. I lie like a seahorse, drunk and swollen. Can't even write on the little board what I'm thinking I want. The hands barely move. The weariness is like a hard sinking into what in my imagination was a giant black womb, and I see myself as someone who can even see sleep.

But scary and terrifying regrets still preserve Moshe my father in black or brown shoes. He always has two pairs, black and brown. He shines them. He pushes strips of thin cardboard he cut from tobacco pouches into both sides of the shoe, smears paste, wipes the brown ones with a brown brush, the black ones with a black brush, and puts the finishing touches on. There's no logic about the way Moshe my father chooses which pair to wear. He wakes up early in the morning, listens to the news on the BBC, reads a little bit of Goethe or Heine, looks at his shoes, which spent the whole night in shoehouses, removes the net from his hair and then something is completely hidden in him. Apparently for no reason, but there does have to be a system. When Mira my sister and I look at his shoes when he's put them on, we know he intended the color he chose, or the color chose him. And where will you find shoehouses today? Who uses a hairbrush today? He's angry at the Poles and Iraqis with their pajamas on the balcony of the house across the street, that was when we lived in Kiryat Meir and he would go at night and hit the garbage can to get rid of the jackals.

And he would say, "The neighbors have wild hair, Yoram," and he said, "Now it's half seven or half eight," and he told me, "I want with you to speak."

He died thirty years ago and I'm lying in the hospital where he died, but not in that same old building, and he's next to me, alive and a lot younger than I am and he tells me, "Yoram, Yoram, the hour is now half seven," and another little moment and another little moment, and he always tells me, "Quite right." I see his soft eyes and don't know what I'm seeing. Nobody I ever knew had such soft eyes as Moshe my father. Sarah my mother had glowing bonfires of eyes, Moshe my father had soft, calm eyes and a kind of deeply rooted gloom, and I feel for the first time in my life, in those last days of mine, I really touch him, understand him, and feel that I'm parting from him because now I'll die along with him and not only against him, like my mother who died against him even though after him, and then the two of us will be dead and we can meet again. I join him and he was seventy-two when he died, while I'm already seventy-five.

Thoughts sail me away from him here in the hospital to our house at 129 Ben Yehuda and Strauss Streets, and I see Yona, the swarthy laughing laundress, sitting for Moshe my father, who didn't understand he could like the body and smell of the Yemenite laundress on the roof, and whenever she'd come to smile at him and sit on the roof and do the laundry he'd find an excuse to go up to the roof, talk with her about the wonderful smell of the laundry soap, and look at her legs spread under the green petticoat that looked like trousers, and here, at the door of the isolation room, I smell the laundry, how I followed her and wanted her to be Moshe my father's lover, after he'd look at my mother and couldn't see her. But suddenly Yona the laundress moves, tells me I'll be a great man, and bends over and lowers down onto the pile and mixes a small bag of bluing in the water boiling from the fire she lit on the big Primus stove that groans and pops, and she wafts the fragrance of a sea anemone I once saw on the shore, smells of lemons and roses, and mixes up the laundry and works hard, sitting with her legs crossed, beating the clothes, stretching them on an ironing board, and Moshe my father stands facing her, doesn't move from her, talks nonsense, and wears a suit, for her, too, and smokes a long twisted pipe that reaches to half the distance between him and her, and she smells the burning tobacco and laughs and tells him, "Fonny, Mr. Kaniuk," and I see that he admires the pungent smell of her cleanliness and everything is so pure and beautiful, and in my mind I sing "Oh Land My Land" and "Lushinka Lushinka" and "Flame on Me Flame" and "Katros Tune" from the show *Dogs by Gorky*, which was always performed on May Day, and "In Silence" and "Autumn Leaves" and "Moscow Nights" and "My Lover" and "Pomegranate Tree" and "Take Me Under Your Wing," as Sarah my mother would sing to me, and "In the songs, "Kalinka Kalinka," "Tulips," "Everything for the Gang," "Between Three and Four," "Oh, bad, it's never been so bad / Suddenly I fell in love with a naked gypsy lad," and I sing, inside myself mainly, "Everything was so beautiful," and "What does it matter it doesn't matter in the villages who dares and if I have bread or if I don't have bread who cares," that's what Shlonsky wrote, me in my head, "with thunderbolts the storm hit them, in the abbreviation of fire sign, signs, signs, and now the storm stands at the edge of the woods and they're shut, too blurred to see." And Penn says that the Land of Israel is mine as it's yours, love of her isn't political, she's the mother of us all, and what if I have bread or if I don't, he was a simple man, thousands were like him, and what was and what I made of my life what does it matter, and I'm with the bastard and naked cancer staying in me and I thought he really would manage to finish me off. Didn't excellent soldiers of the Arab Legion try to finish me off? Literary critics tried. Settlers tried. So what do I have to fear from a cancer riding on ants that will bite me?

Suddenly I leave the hospital and stand with a group of young men dressed in white sailors' uniforms by a red bus my father used to sing about, "On the Sabbath there's no newspaper, no red bus, no school by day or night, the park is shut up tight." A great poet like Alterman he wasn't. The red bus was a "Ma'avir," which today is "Dan," and soon we'll call the company BIG because to stupid Israelis that sounds in both eyes is blurred. We meet and check each other out. Our old eyes. They won't fool us. They understand right away who is sick and with what. They also discern the time. It's recorded on our faces. They try to know who will die first, me or him. If he dies first, I'll have to go to his funeral, and it's just like him to die in a heat wave, he always did try to screw things up for everybody, we'll wander around in a heat wave to bury him in some distant graveyard and we'll look at others. Aryeh's sick, he knows, we know, he plays the game, not really he but everybody, and I'm sorry for him, he was once so young and so handsome. And another wonderful line by Penn suddenly comes up in me, "Fever of *khamsins*," and I look straight ahead, across from me stands the old and bruised me, and also the young men we once were, and Aryeh sings, "Aryeh, Aryeh, get up and volunteer for the Hebrew battalion." I feel that, whether or not that happened, our singing together in this land was a kind of glue. Religion. It's the synagogue.

I look. Miranda is sleeping. She's tired, poor thing. I'm driving her crazy with my silence and my plea for her to be with me here all the time, and my sister Mira, whose eyes are also shut, and my Naomi, who does me so many favors. And I think that the shared weeping of the Land of Israel in songs, mainly Russian ones, that we grew up on and sang with Hasidic devotion—my parents, our parents were Hasids, how far can you go? I try to remember. Where am I?

And if I'm here in the hospital how come I was now the one across from the splendid thirteenth-century cathedral on the Frishman corner of Dizengoff, Frishman, who wrote stories of the desert in the fields of Poland and knew the smell of desolation and the *wadis* in the streets of Warsaw, and when the War of Liberation ended, and today I'm not sure it really happened, we went to besieged Jerusalem and shouted, "If we die, bury us in the mountains of Ba'ab-el-Wad," and the old *yekke* with the cap of the citizen patrol would say, "Quiet, boys, you won't die in Ba'ab-el-Wad, you'll die here, on Jaffa Road," and we said with devotion and sadness that after the war we'd meet in a phone booth in Mughrabi Square, next to the fat yekke sausage vendor, and to get a sausage you always had to tell him that Goethe was greater than Shakespeare, and the office called "The Office to Care for Soldiers Who Left Their Units Not by Their Own Fault" was there.

Suddenly I see Miranda's beautiful eyes and it appears to me. A tent, round, in Tel Yosef, and on the canvas of the tent, one Amos wrote, "I am the glow, I am the splendor, I who sign below, Amos the Pompous Fool." And we came to the office on Allenby Street straight from the phone booth on Mughrabi, right after Jerusalem and the battles and the dead, and we went into the room and there were papers where a doctor in Jerusalem had written details about my wound, and on the spot they recruited us into the new army, which was already called the Israel Defense Force, and at that very moment they discharged us from that army and gave us seven pounds of payment to cover the months we had fought, and we went to Café Pilz and sang with Menashke, the son of a rabbi, those songs that didn't stop sawing away in my mind, and they were like a fever of khamsins and how come I didn't know that line then?

Miranda wakes up. Naomi is sitting next to me. Silence. I slept. Naomi remembers the eve of Memorial Day a few days or a week ago. I lay confused, the wheels of the destroyed mind gritted their teeth in the factory, I'm awake and asleep at one and the same time, and I don't know about what or for what, suddenly the siren for the eve of Memorial Day sounds. Apparently I felt a kind of connection to something greater than me and from that hospital, from my friggin' death, I sang in my mind, with some cheek, "They took to the Mountains of Ephraim a new young victim," and Naomi remembers that when the Memorial Day siren sounded, I shook, I couldn't stand up, and Naomi says I tried to raise one hand and how, in the end, I did manage to stretch my hand a little, a fraction of an inch; she says tears flowed from my eyes and I remember now that the tears flowed slowly and crept through clefts of the dark, and for a moment I came out of the place where I was.

Naomi says that was touching, how I tried to salute my dead comrades from the Harel Brigade. I tell her in my heart who I saluted. Menahem, Sus, Nahum Arieli, whom I saw killed at the Kastel, and Posa, the hero, son of Poznanski, an intellectual Jew, and Amos the stupid and Yashka the partisan.

I really miss Yashka. He had a warmth and a smile and an ancient, historical wisdom that we in the Land of Israel didn't have. We didn't know that it's impossible to really live without roots or history, and Yashka, if he had lived, would have been close to eighty today, but he remains forever a wonderful young man of twenty. He ascended to the Land in an illegal ship, went to Cyprus, managed to get out, trained for two days, and came to us somehow. He was so handsome with his dark blue eyes, and would sing Russian songs and even knew a few words of Hebrew and was a hero and a demon of destruction, and I also called him Yashka Skinny Mule, and he would make me laugh when he straightened up like an idiot and shot standing up like some Jewish cowboy from the armored vehicle and fought with a courage we had never known, and sometimes we happened to fight together, he and I, and in one of the battles, maybe in Bayt Mahsir, maybe in the San Simon monastery, I saw that he was wounded, he twitched from a bullet that hit his head and very slowly folded over and blood flowed like a small cascade, and he fell straight down, and he knelt and fell over and on his destroyed and bleeding face there was still a charming smile, and I put my face to his chest, and tried to make him breathe, but there was no pulse, and I was angry that he had betrayed me, he could have lived, I wanted him to be my friend outside that shitty place, too, but he was dead.

I went with his body to Kibbutz Kiryat Anavim in an armored vehicle. I carried him in a blanket, and Rafi and Tibi helped me carry him and we put him in the opening of the tent and from there to the graveyard we had dug even before the battle. All of them wanted to sleep but they waited for me to bury him, they were tired, and I said I wanted to give them what they wanted, but I was very angry, I said he didn't deserve to die yet and I said like a scolded baby that they weren't half the man he was. There was in his presence a kind of dreadful need to live and bring back so many days that were lost, and I didn't let anyone do what they would do to those who were killed before being buried, I didn't let them take his clothes, I didn't let M take off his Stalingrad watch that he got after the battles there, or the medal they said he got after he killed a German in "Roosha," and then we remembered that from so much bereavement and weariness we forgot to ask him his full name and all we knew was that he was called Yashka Partisan. We were supposed to bury him as "Anonymous," solitary he wasn't anymore, and with whatever strength I had left, I ran up the mountain to Beit Fefferman and asked Yitzhak Rabin to let me write on the wooden strip over the grave "Yashka Partisan" instead of "Anonymous," and Yitzhak Rabin agreed.

I thought of his unjust death. And of my funny death, which at my age is just. Yashka wasn't from here. He didn't owe anything to the Hebrew Yishuv in the Land of Israel, and he wasn't killed in Stalingrad, but here in this war, and for him our war was a Mickey Mouse war and he came to fight against a few Arabs who shouted when they shot, and he stayed with us for maybe a month and didn't know our songs. He didn't know who Ussishkin was, didn't know who Berl Repetur was, not even who Abraham Shapiro was or Berla Shvayger or Trumpeldor, and death is the wisdom of the body to forget life and pain, and with him death erased his ascent from his bereavement there to the Land of Israel that would bury him.

And then I fall asleep and think that Yashka is waiting for me dead in the next room, waiting for a proper burial. Naomi leaves. Maybe it's already another day. Mira my sister sits and says I'm the only brother she has and I should recover. At the moment I don't seem to know where I am and I hear from somebody that today is May Day. Or maybe the night of May Day. And the night of May Day is the seventy-fifth anniversary of my birth. I fall asleep and wake up and hear mixed-up words. I lie in bed and see a tombstone in front of me. I see only its back, blurred, heavy, clumsy, but somehow I also see the front side. There's no writing on the tombstone. Only wiped-out symbols. A pale old illustration of a dove with a fish in her mouth, like illustrations I used to make.

In my pillow here, in the hospital, a hole gapes open. My head lands deep in the hole. In front of me, I see the tombstone, and I shout without a voice for them to take it away from me. I hear music, I hear singing, and it seems to be two floors below me, I hear Miranda explaining to somebody I can't see, and I don't recognize his voice, and somebody says to Miranda, "Hey, how is he? Is he alive?" And Miranda says something that doesn't reach my ear, and he says, "Years ago, in New York," and I recognize the voice but not the owner of the voice, and he says to Miranda, "It was May Day and we were in Union Square, there was an assembly of Communists and Reds, and there was an old couple there, Alex and Sonya, and they had a Russian restaurant on Eleventh Street across from a Jewish cemetery, next to the balcony on the first floor, and they were singing enthusiastically, she not so much, she told me she was a Zionist and wore a pinafore and held a Keren Kayemet box, and little Alex held a picture of Stalin and mounted police hit them and they sang, and Pete Seeger and his Weavers, they heard a record by Paul Robeson and waved red flags, and mobs of people were angry and fat people with strong faces and dreadful anger in their eyes spat on them, and there were beatings, and Yoram ran to rescue his wife, Lee Baker, who stood in the square and sang the Internationale, and she laughed at the sight of him and shouted contemptuously and looked at Sonya who was it wears a brown stone caftan topped with a big kippa, and I'm not sure anymore that it's really mine.

I hear people singing in the distance. I want to sing, too. Suddenly a funnel gang bursts into the room from the naval course at Sdot Yam, the Fields of the Sea, and one of them is swimming in the sea, and where there was a field there's now sea, and a funnel gang from Course Nine sings, "Shoshanna Shoshanna Shoshanna, the moon rises over a cloud" and "Put in her mouth put in her mouth put in her mouth a broomstick" and "Samara hop hop" and "She'll come without pajamas she'll come, she'll come without pajamas she'll come" and such educated songs and the singer Adi shrieks, and Haim Gouri looks sad and reads a poem by Alterman and is disappointed that I don't remember the poem and suddenly the Carmon chorus, just now back from a tour abroad, bursts into the place. The girls aren't the embarrassed youngsters they once were, with the smiles stuck onto their faces with carpenters' glue, now they're old, made up as they were then, a typical Israeli makeup they explained to the uncircumcised in America was part of the Pioneer tradition mixed with the biblical, they wear pinafores and long skirts because they circulated in the world and, with admirable ungainliness, they dance "Hora Nahalal" and "The Pomegranate Tree Gave Its Smell" and everything gets confused, they dance and Haim Gouri leaves, and the funnel gang is killed in a battle on the road to Jerusalem, and suddenly Dr. Dayan comes to me to remove a bandage and smiles, and I'm shaken, apparently I was hallucinating again, but that was real, it has to be.

Miranda comes and tells me happy birthday, my darling, and kisses me, and so does Naomi, and so does my sister, and so does a sweet Russian nurse, who chuckles and says, "What, he's not young? What, he's really seventy-five years old?" Sweet. I try to live up to the event, as they say in English, and try without a voice to say a word about my birthday, and think, "Wait a minute, Kaniuk, what's so happy about a birthday?" And I say in a whisper, "Your beauty, Miranda, is a divine axiom." When we met forty-six years ago, you must remember, we went to the movies on Forty-Second Street, we saw two films, one was Bergman's *The Seventh Seal*, and between that film and the next, I trembled, I was in love and I told you you'd be the mother of my daughter, and we'd get married, and you were seventeen and you said yes twice. And I went to your parents, I said I was a Jew, divorced, and made frozen falafel with friends. And they looked at me in dreadful amazement. They smiled. They drank infinite quantities of bourbon. And I never believed somebody could really love me, not even you. You were too young to know if you loved me, maybe I charmed you with my sea stories and my war stories, or my bartender stories, and maybe essentially with my otherness, creating last pictures, writing a ridiculous book, and my friends in the café on Ninety-First and Broadway made bets on how long we'd last, the longest they gave was eight months. And I did have a hundred and one women and never believed any of them loved me. Karen Blixen, one of my favorite authors, tells of a rich old Russian surrounded by beautiful women who prance around him, and he's asked if he thinks they love him, and he answers that he's got a chef who makes him excellent omelets and he doesn't ask him if he loves him.

And only now, Miranda—after all the operations, after forty-six years of life together, and they weren't always easy, sometimes quite cruel and impossible, and there was poverty, and I was drunk for years, and I acted up and I left you and I saw you weeping at night, and there wasn't anything to eat in the house and I took the little bit of money to buy awful 777 Brandy and they cut off the electricity because I didn't pay and they cut off the gas and the phone, and you stood and wept because you had to kill mosquitoes that filled the house and kill them with Flit, and you wept because you didn't want to kill living things, and Aya went to sell ice cream on the beach in Herzliya so there would be money in the house, and I was a shitty father and a shitty husband and a shitty man—only now, here in my sickbed, as they say, did I learn something I didn't know and that excites me, and maybe more than anything surprises me, I learned that you have really and truly loved me for forty-seven years ever since we met and forty-six years since we married.

I smile but you stand weeping at my bed. Dr. Szold passes by and examines me and tells you, "He'll be fine," and you don't see that smile of love. Downstairs, at the party for me, somebody is singing and I am singing along in my heart, and we're singing, I'm singing songs in my mind, "Oh mother mother why, why, oh why did you give me life" and "At the fifty-seventh blow Katrina still didn't die" and "Why do you trample on my grave" and "Believe a day will come" and "I move and you're far away" and "Sleep valley, the splendid land" in the pure voice and clear Hebrew of Sarah my mother. I feel death flowing into me and from me and from the dead bodies of my neighbors who are no longer, since I saw orderlies come in to make the beds for new patients waiting to get into this slaughterhouse. But I'm not in the regular ICU anymore, I'm in isolation, and aside from me, sometimes, it's only the poor rabbi-teacher-doctor who's shrieking.

A person is born to betray, I thought, and no betrayal can exist without love, and no love can exist without hidden betrayal. I once loved someone the Hebrew Yishuv called "the jewel," Yosef Lishansky, who was also called Tubin from Metulla, and, according to his slanderers, he would preen and adorn himself, and, according to those lemons of the Land of Israel, he would scour himself, and never mind now the whole story with Sarah Aaronsohn, who was attracted to him and he to her, and the good-for-nothings of "Nili," the darlings of the Land of Israel with their French, who teased Sarah about her love for Yosef, but in the end, he was their real hero and it was he who was taken to Khan El Basha in Damascus and hanged and all that night he slept on his clothes so they'd look ironed and he stood in the square with a sign hanging on his neck and covering his body, "This is what is done to a traitor in Turkey," and he said in a loud voice as he was hanged, "I didn't betray you, rotten Ottomans, because before betrayal there has to be love, and we didn't love you."

And from the abyss of anger I felt I heard the song "Blue Shirt Better than All the Jewels" and "Red Flag Rising on High," and in the center I see a delicate flame lit with a light of glory, see the heavy heat wave lying on Tel Aviv like a giant black mountain and the fever of khamsins outside the hospital, see the noise, see the Eduard Bernstein Street corner of Lassalle with the labor activists' little houses, see the lemon trees and the orange trees and the sand and the yekkes building a three-story house in the khamsin and singing, "Who will build, will build a house in Tel Aviv? We the pioneers," and every single one of them was a doctor in Germany or an engineer or a violinist, and then they sing lieder by Schubert and Schumann. And I see Rosa Cohen, Yitzhak Rabin's mother, walking on Ben Yehuda and Strauss Streets corner of Lassalle, with a giant smile, courage in her eyes, hoisting a red flag stuck under her belt and over her lowered skirt, chirping a song of toil, and somebody sings, "Kfar Szold will be a young kibbutz tomorrow, countless members." And then I'm almost awake and I sing, "Rise up, shake off oppression, nation of slaves and starving" and "Give the floor to Comrade Parabellum, free speech to Comrade Submachine Gun" and "The roar of the cannons is silent, the battlefield is orphaned," and what is an orphaned battlefield anyway? Do I feel I hear those words I feel? Do I remember my birth taking place now, at dawn, on May 2, my birthday on the night of the workers' holiday? I remember but don't remember what I remember. Is the life I came back to the life I wanted to come back to? Was I really in it before? Is there a memory of the days before waking? Can it be that I came from a narrow eternity, and like the poet I searched for my coming before the world was created? Maybe that's what was explained to me in the back of my mind, and so this is the eve of my birthday.

I still see the tombstone before me. On the back is carved 1930, the year I was born. Nothing else. Not the day of my death. On top of the tombstone is an uncarved stone ring with a shtreimel on it, and on the shtreimel is a giant dome. The tombstone brings me a bliss I have never known. Maybe because I think self-righteously that this is an indication of when I came and when I finished, and what was between them can be counted.

understand whether the tombstone is mine and know that in its place downstairs the noise and the ringing and the shouts go on, and somehow I see through the floor how they're making the birthday party there and Adi Etzion is now singing a song from an opera by Monteverdi that Moshe my father loved. There are other people here. They stand on three stories, but somebody in my mind is explaining to me that today they really bury in three-story mausoleums, so why not me, on my seventy-fifth birthday, and here of all places, like the beautiful young men who were murdered on the way to Gush Etzion and somebody organized a Palmach celebration and made a bonfire in the hospital. They sent around a jar they called a *finjan* and somebody played Duke Ellington's "Take the A Train," and I heard Abdul Vaha'ab sing "Besame Mucho," sung in Hebrew by Abdul Mahrof, and I hear the Andrews Sisters singing "*Bei mir bist du sheyn*," and the goings-on downstairs scare me, I wanted to surprise them and die before my birthday and what now, what will they do with me alive? I want to tell them I couldn't come to the celebration because I'm busy being buried, and that I'll die on my birthday, and I promised somebody that's how it would be, but who? It's easier to die than to be born, but they're busy partying and don't pay attention to the logic.

A big woman, who looks like the maid Zahava who washed me in the tub, stands up straight at the celebration and trills, and I try to turn her attention to the announcement

I found on a tree in the street and hung in my house above the table: "Ohra's mother betrayed our trust. If you're different and pushing forty-five, handsome, six-foot-three, someone is waiting for you." Well, I'm here and not at home, and I'm much shorter. And the woman goes on singing. And Adi Etzion cackles as she clears her throat and Haim Gouri comes back, apparently he came with people I once knew but not anymore, they're the ones who made the bonfire of "Around around the finjan," and people try to move things along, to bring me a birthday present, and Miranda, you sat and looked at me with your love that looked like a fire disguised in the thin silk I brought you from the trip to China, and it is exciting to see your love really come and go out to me and return from me and alight on your face. My body is dead, my sweet, and I can't show you the excitement.

Look, Miranda, I'm not writing to strangers, I'm writing to me, to you, to Naomi, and to Aya. I, who took you from your people, your homeland, your father's house, your God, your culture, and brought you to this hole in Palestine, Land of Israel, such a small state whose name can be written on the map only on the sea, and it—the state I fought to establish—isn't willing to grant you the rights it grants to everyone who comes from Tunisia or Georgia because he or she is circumcised and you, Miranda, not you.

Somebody approaches the bed. I don't know him. Tall and handsome, looks like an intellectual and says he's from the

Ministry of Agriculture and asks if I remember him from the kindergarten of Haya Broyde, Brenner's wife, and it's been more than seventy years since we attended her kindergarten on Bograshov Street. I peep at the photo he takes out of the briefcase and shows me, I'm sitting cross-legged in it and smiling. I don't remember him. Nice of him to come visit me. Yitzhak Shiloh comes, too. I haven't seen him in years. He sits next to me and tells about the days when we knew each other years and years ago, and like my big Aunt Sarah, I make a list of those who didn't come and those who did, and like big Sarah, I don't forgive those who didn't come to visit me, even if they're dead.

All I can think of to keep from singing over and over in my mind "Blue shirt and it costs," is that I would have wanted not to be born retroactively. I see the birth clearly. If I remember correctly, it was the most subjective happening that happened to me, and I think about the moments of grace and the moments of wonder and the moments of shame, in no clear order. Among the songs of the loop playing nonstop in my head I am once again at my birthday and think how one moment can change your whole life. How Professor Halperin said, "Yoram, you've got cancer," and everybody talks about fate, can fate explain a moment when your whole life suddenly changes?

In the last operation, there was a moment when I declined and a moment when I was eighteen and the British soldier serving in the Arab Legion shot me from the wall in Jerusalem and my whole world became a narrow space between the blue eye on the wall and the muzzle close to me, and then I died, and death became life because two or three minutes passed and I didn't feel dead. And there was something greater than fear in me. A soldier kills and is killed, and I was easy prey and he had to kill me, that's the law of wars, but the second shot didn't come. The two happenings, that one and this one now, are connected to one another, and the moment that's two or three weeks old in my death in the ICU, unconscious, in a coma, or however it's called, is bound up with the moment of Jerusalem. Maybe the British officer on the walls of Jerusalem pictured Jesus's resurrection when he shot me once and didn't shoot me a second time. Why didn't he shoot me a second time? Something happened, he decided to be God and to spare me, at least until my death at the age of seventy-five in Ichilov hospital.

And I thought about what I had done in the life I was given. About my art. I never succeeded in doing the art I should have done. I had models that were hard to compete with or to carry on in their way. My art was hard for me. I was always crippled with an amazing inability and a need to be only myself and was sorry I wasn't different, and what I did wasn't right. In some objective sense, my ability was limited.

I studied drawing because it was easy for me. I wondered quite a bit about my success in drawing. Success? Hard to call it that, but it was like success. I was very young and didn't deserve praise. I was imprisoned in helplessness and couldn't get over it.

In my youth I wanted to be like everyone else. I couldn't. The pockets full of marbles didn't stick out enough under the short pants, the sandals looked different from everybody else's, they laughed at me, I decided to be born in Germany because I loved the sad grace of the German children who came back then. I forced myself to yell "Ooow" when I was attacked because the children of the Land of Israel shouted "Aaay," and the children decided to mock me and attacked me next to the Turkish fort on Ben Yehuda Street and I fought and they hit me hard and yelled "Aooo" and then Amihud bruised my ribs and I yelled "Yaaaa." My childhood was an attempt to be somebody else. I wrote in secret; I was ashamed of the watercolors I painted at the Yarkon River; when everyone went to fuck Rina Pakoski from behind, and afterward they said she married an Arab or an Englishman, I didn't go; and when they went to Gan Rina movie house, to sneak in by climbing over high fences, I went with them because I was a Zionist and Zionism was us, to be like everyone else.

I climbed over the high fence next to Ben Yehuda Street across from the community center in Gan Rina, what a beautiful movie house that was, on summer evenings, a wind blew from the sea and my conscience pricked me and I went to the other side and went down and came in with them, but they went into the movie house, which was open to the sea, and I went out to buy a ticket for eleven cents. The bastards waited for me and said I'd never be like Buck Jones or heroes of the Berla Shveyger Guard or Portugali or Alexander Zaïd from Sheikh Abrek. I dreamed of being a bold farmer, I went to study mechanical metalworking, I had zero talent, but I was the only one who passed with flying colors the psychotechnical test they gave us on Bialik Street and the man who administered the test claimed I was a mechanical genius. In vocational school in Haifa I didn't understand a thing about mechanics, I was bad in crafts, I loved history, which was a default choice, and after two years they told my mother that I was promoted but not in our school—I was the first one they tried that formulation on.

All I wanted was what I couldn't do, and what I could do I was ashamed of. When I worked as a sailor on *Pan York* and brought thousands of Holocaust survivors to Israel at the end of the War of Independence, everyone else went to whores in Naples and Marseilles, I would sit beloved by the Diaspora children in the transit camp. I loved the Jews, even though we had learned for many years that the Jews were a wretched, unredeemable, and stooped people and went like sheep to the slaughter, and only in the Land of Israel would the new Jew emerge, offspring of Joshua, Nimrod,

My failure was that I painted and wrote not as I wanted not to write, but as I had to. I couldn't be clearer, nicer, and, to tell the truth, I'm still a writer by default.

Helplessness isn't only a powerful instrument, it is also dangerous. I was fed up with my self-hatred, fed up with the arrogance of my need to wallow in dangers, but I told myself that I had already lived enough, that I had done what others don't do in ten chapters of life and I don't need to go on living, that because of the prostate operation I had ten years ago I can't have any more children, I don't know how to have fun, and what does a person need, as the Indians say, but to sire a son, build a house, and plant a tree. I sired two daughters, planted a Jewish Agency tree, and didn't build a house, but a rented apartment is also a house.

Until the age of thirteen, I had a babysitter on nights when my parents went out. I was afraid of the dark. I was afraid of swallowing. I was afraid of closed places. I was afraid of high places. I was afraid of everything. I was afraid of how I looked. I was afraid of my thoughts. I was afraid of weakness. I volunteered for the Palmach at the age of seventeen and from the beginning I was afraid, but when the war broke out I fought all right, I didn't have the courage to be afraid and I lacked a fear of fighting in fear. I remember how Yitzhak Rabin came down from Beit Fefferman on Ma'ale HaHamisha and asked, "Who's this Kaniuk here?" And they told him it was I and he told me, "Listen, kid, what? You want to be a sapper?" Because I would run like a fool into the fire, as if I were marked out, and at the same time, would shake with fear, and I saved a comrade I moved away from me to be exposed to the bullets instead of him, but after an hour he died and I didn't. In the battle for the Kastel, my buddies in the platoon died. I was left alone. Even the names of my buddies there I don't remember anymore. I sat on the grass in Kibbutz Kiryat Anavim and didn't know where to go. Somebody I didn't know came and asked how I was and I told him and he said to me, "What are you complaining about, sit here, sleep here tonight in the hay loft and don't go to battle all night." He scared me not to go out and not to take risks and he took me to the unit of the terrific robber reservists and I rewarded myself for all the horrible desires in me, for the need "simply to do that," as the Americans say.

There was in me the need to hitch my wagon to a star, like Nietzsche, and I thought I'd surprise because I didn't know how to walk. I thought I'd act in my own way and be loved because I was a good writer, even if I only knew how not to write. I knew how to write differently because not only did the acceptable disgust me but it was hard for me. In the end, what you're reading now is also somehow a book. Somebody might ask, "How's the book?" You'll tell him the book is quite nice, even interesting, a little depressing, too bad it wasn't shortened, it's a bad book, a wild book, the book isn't well written or edited enough, and somebody else will say there's much imprecision here and mistakes should probably have been corrected, but I'm not a writer of "probably," and what there is is all I can do.

The chronicles of my life are a meaningless event I tried to condense into unashamed meaning. I have a hard time with the aesthetic perspective of all that was horrible. Is Goya's execution beautiful? I feel now for the first time in my life that I'm touching something that is the secret of my existence. The secret is simple and banal—there's no meaning to my life or to anybody else's life. Maybe when I died I came to God and saw what I had always imagined God to be, and He's not only what is right but what isn't right, so everybody wants to appease Him. And I thought, How do we know the dead, how do we know tears? And do the tears, like the fingernails, go on growing even after the body is extinguished?

Late at night, after I wrote and read those sentences, I woke up from a quick nap and remembered vaguely what the doctors wanted me to forget in the operation. That was the only memory I had during the last operation. I saw myself cut open. The Japanese fish looking sadly at those eating his living flesh. I knew my eyes saw the pieces the doctors were taking out and putting in. I didn't feel pain. In my condition, pain is a gift, because it's a sign of life. When that sight comes back to me I want to laugh at how dreadful but wonderful it is that I see myself cut open, as in the Middle

Ages when people were killed slowly so they could see their own death. It's sealed in me, that sight.

The Talmud says that a dream is a closed letter and the interpretation is always that of the other. I lay dying, not here in the hospital, but at the sea. Always I return to the sea. And then I dream that I'm going to the sea and parking my fucked-up Peugeot 309 at the windowpane factory. I look here and there, go into a busy and warm café where the waves are breaking. The murmur of the water soothes me. To drink coffee by the waves and go out, and I go out and the car's not there. Golda Meir passes by on a scooter, wearing a helmet made of a woman's bathing cap, rubber with a picture of the sea on it, and somebody gives me an injection and yells. Maybe a doctor comes. He says something and they run to connect me to a gas balloon, I'm choking but starting to breathe, and rise up and go with Golda Meir, she lives near the house of Sarah my mother, behind Brodetski Street. And on the street near the sea there's a lot of traffic, the street is full of water, but people are sitting in the middle of the street on white plastic chairs and the waves reach them. Suddenly Sidney Poitier stands up and yells. I approach and he asks me with an evil, ironic smile how Charlie Parker is. Golda tells him, "You're finished, Poitier! For three minutes of a diaper ad you came to Israel?" I ask Golda what's been bothering me all the time, "What happened to our friendship? What have you got against me?"

She says it's all because of the clocks. We're next to a phone booth, and I'm worried about the car. "What to do?" I ask. "Call," Golda says. "Who?" I ask. "The insurance company!" she answers. "I thought first the police," I say, but all my papers are in the car and everything is gray. A sharp thin sun shines. People dressed in suits, in the words of Teacher Blich, "are cavorting" at the sea, and I sit down immediately and write a poem about a woman who sings in Bethlehem to old women bragging about their terrific grandchildren who managed to climb the ladder of promotion as commanders of the Roman army, and she sings, "My grandson wasn't a Roman officer, he was God and was crucified by your sons!" Nobility is the last thing to be found in human beings. In fish and butterflies there is nobility, but not in human beings. I become the shadow of myself and I'm choking. Feel that I have no air. I open my eyes and a nurse is standing over me and asking what happened. I touch my body and weep at how old and ugly it looks.

Never could I see from the bed the switch of the air conditioner at the end of the room, and I ask the nurse who looks like a frog, a sweet man who always looked scared, I signal with grimaces to turn on the air conditioner. A heavy silence, a network of machinations. I don't know where the word "machinations" came from, but "probably" it rose up from the depths of my mind, and if it came, that's a sign it had to come. I look at a pigeon on the window and I seem to remember it or its family. When I was a young man, I'd walk to the Arab village of Somail, and some of its ruined houses still stand at the corner of Arlozorov and Ibn Gabirol Street, not far from Ichilov, and on one of them a long pair of jeans is stretched, and right here, downstairs, I and my best friend Amos would buy sorghum seeds for our pigeons, which nested in our dovecote on Halperin Street near the Muslim graveyard. So, the pigeon on my window must be an offspring of the Arab pigeon and so is also a pigeon of the Nakba, speaking only Arabic, dreaming of Palestine, of the end of Zionism, of lifting the occupation, and since I fell in love with a pigeon I call her big Sarah after my wicked and beautiful aunt, and I look at her, an Arabic pigeon before she became a Palestinian, and she's been here for many generations, and that's all I can see in this friggin' place called Ichilov that once, when I was a boy, was a padlock called Gordon for British officers to ride horses.

I couldn't figure out what side of the new building of Ichilov I was on and what I was looking at, on Dafna and Henrietta Szold Street or on the courthouse and the museum. The window is all I saw except for the room itself. Hours crawled by when I looked at the window that framed a world for me. On the windowsill I had Palestinian pigeons from Sumail of the Nakba putting on a charming striptease and cleaning their feathers with heroic and tranquil daintiness, shaking them out, leaping, and coming back, cheeping a little, day after day. At night I watched the play of lights of Tel Aviv. In the early evening, there's still a little bit of light left. Then the light grows dim. And then it's almost night, but the lights in the houses fall silent. The lights give way, the houses grow dark, and darkness comes. In the dark hundreds of lighted and wiped-out windows are seen. Here and there a flicker. A tiny plane slices through the clouds and it's impossible to see it. The evening that falls makes me sad. I want to plead. I have no one to plead to and nothing to plead for. Miranda and Naomi and Mira aren't here this evening. I look at my pigeons. They're used to me. Now they're not just Palestinians, now they want to be *shahids* against me and for justice. They demand the right of return. What is the value of my little bit of suffering against the dying of a Druse woman who is now yelling and weeping in the next room. She is entitled to weep. And she's so young and not old like me, and she'll die the day after tomorrow. Who needs this life with diseases? There's nothing more frustrating in the cells of those doomed to the ICU than the inability to be understood by those around you.

Miranda does try. She comes back. The night ends somehow and she asks with her softness, "You want some air? There's a problem with breathing? You want me to call somebody for you? It hurts? Where?" My pain is indifferent to me. My body doesn't explain itself. Friends stand who know I'm dying and they weep. They wear the clothes that defend from that snake, from the fatal virus lying in wait for me and destroying my lungs, and it's contagious and they have to wear over their clothes a kind of muslin gown and a muslin hat and muslin shoes, and they wear that covering with an apologetic smile because it's not nice for them to appear like that, but they must say to themselves, "Compared to what he's going through, what's my suffering," and I see on their faces a silly sense of victory mixed with pity that, to feel good and to feel healthy, they come to suffer with me for themselves, too, and I laugh at the sight of the cloth they have to wear. Beyond the screen, I see their tears, a real performance perhaps, but mostly it's fear of what they see, and the feeling that they're healthy may be against me a little, and I think in my pettiness that I understand that they came to say goodbye to me, but I'm almost alive, and after they've been told I died it's a little disappointing for them that I'm still alive, and they're angry at themselves, but proximity to death engenders guilt in healthy people and they came to view the performance of my death, and I'm not dead before their eyes but writhing in life and descending from the slope of the fatal patient and even go on living, and they don't know that I'm clinging to life like a hawk to its corpse.

Ever since the wound in the battles in Jerusalem I've been depressed. At the age of seventy-five, in the middle of the death that took up residence in me with the cancer and wanted to defeat me, for the first time in my life, I came out of the shellshock I was in for so many years. Connecting the two minutes at Mount Zion with the dying at Ichilov healed me. They say in English, *He is a real person*. The word *person* comes from the word "persona" and means he's a real mask of himself. So I'm waiting for myself defeated at the end of the story and taking off the mask.

The first thing that happened after "Yoram, wake up" and after the forgetting in the coma was the sense of dimmed light in the place where I was and didn't know I was there. I don't know if it was then or a few days later. I understood that Mira my sister, who helped me so much, and a beautiful woman she is, and sad, and her sons and grandsons were here, she loves me. Friends were here. I understood that Miranda, the enigmatic and indecipherable woman who, after all those years with her, I know less about than I know about Mordechai from the corner grocery, she loves me. She's a person who has no explanation. No person I've known in my life has been as indecipherable as she. She doesn't explain herself, is unexpected, she's delicate as wax and yet strong, she doesn't wear makeup, doesn't go to the hairdresser, cuts her own hair, doesn't go to a beauty salon or a gym, doesn't do cosmetic care, she loves to wander in the city and buy secondhand clothes, loves to give to everyone in need, is dreadfully honest, absolutely generous, and suddenly I'm transmuted into a beloved man—in a comfortable, nice sense. I wasn't there before, I wasn't myself but only a chance and a thought, and I choked with happiness, and then nails were driven into my throat. Blood came into my throat. There was blood in my mouth. I spat myself into what I was, and there was in me phlegm of torments from that not-knowing of my nothingness and inability to love me that suddenly burst.

I see nurses stretching over me and a doctor's with them. Somebody seems to be trying to adjust my feeding tube, and it hurts. Suddenly I have no air and I'm choking and they're bandaging me, and I'm writhing in pain without moving and asking without a voice, "Where is Golda Meir?" But I have no voice. One nurse says, "You're so lucky to have a woman like Miranda," and my body becomes hot and I look at the nurse and he winks at me and says, "Your sister is a beautiful woman. Your daughter Naomi is terrific, she's beautiful and smart and good, like your wife." In my eyes, women were always beautiful in black-and-white, without ideas, but in color they scared me. I loved to visit their womanly limbs, but I couldn't look at them, I loved them in satin dresses, regal, arrogant, nodding. I wrote poems about them. They didn't read. Art can't be ethical.

*

And a while later, I felt strange longings for the cancer that had stayed in me for years and led me to danger and was cut out with knives and monstrous instruments I could only glance at for a few seconds before the first operation of blessed memory. And now it's 2007, about a year and a half has passed since the operations. I think of those days, I really don't understand what I'm looking for and what really happened to me, and I want to correct something that may have broken down at age eighteen in Jerusalem, on a March day that was beautiful and warm and clear and pure and full of blood and dread, full of pits, full of scorched flesh, full of corpses and hopes and Orthodox Jews waving white flags of surrender, and I want to turn the pigeons from Somail into Palestinian refugees and us into their brutal heirs and I can, if only I want, buy sorghum seed straight from myself, and I'm deluding myself again.

I always lived on the razor's edge, but I swallowed it wrapped in bittersweet chocolate. I was cut inside myself, but the cut had a bittersweet taste. Sarah my mother shed tears, that's what she would say angrily when she was angry at me. I dream and hallucinate to the Palestinian pigeons about the fucking isolation and suddenly a clock is hanging there. The clock is diamond shaped and has a lot of numbers, more than the normal twenty-four hours. The watch face is slightly crooked and the hour is sometimes 3:15 and sometimes 4:15, and in the distance I see the nurses running here and there and I twitch but they don't see. The sorrow is solid and only a few nurses look at me but they don't see a thing. Shouts here and there. And the noise of monitors and the slicing lights that look like strips of light from outer space, and the nights are still gloomy. The space ships go on their mysterious way through the wall on the backs of people paralyzed in silence before the monitors. I see them. I don't know who they are. Our God, who can't bear meat with milk and scorches it to extinction, He's the most satanic of possible creators, but not exactly forgiven, and He pees on me in my sickbed that I may not get out of. All my life I've worked on a search for a faith that has no connection with God, I've relied on the idea that the concepts of "knowing" and "believing" are opposed.

There won't be another opportunity. Perhaps the blood that was flowed into me is full of AIDS. My mother gave birth to me in spite of everything just so I'd hear the beating of her heart. I knew I had an ancient connection with the moment when I was formed, but I have felt it mainly since my illness, because in illness, that moment becomes much more familiar, becomes understood, maybe also more malicious, and I, who am I who dared to be born in Freund Hospital on Yehuda Halevi Street because of one moment of love of Moshe my father for Sarah my mother, and I'm lying stricken and dreaming about myself with a kind of strange and yearning hindsight.

Suddenly I'm not in the hospital. I'm lying in bed, in my parents' apartment at 129 Ben Yehuda and Strauss, in the winter, the wind is hitting the shutters, the pounding of the righteous sea sounds like a drum roll, and I smell the fragrance of the gutters. I loved their humming and the wailing of the cats between the downpours and I would hide under the down comforter, in the cold room, disguised as Emil the Detective or the Count of Monte Cristo in his cell, on his island near Marseilles, where I later visited when I was a sailor, and it felt nice to be imprisoned under the blanket, cut off from the world where Sarah my mother and Moshe my father slept in separate rooms and Moshe my father listened to the BBC to know what exactly was happening in Leningrad and what was happening in the siege of Moscow or Stalingrad. I would make up reality and I still do. My life was a blend of what happened and how I improve, change, build plots. My whole life was an invention of a story that was true but also not, that was legends, always truth, not always right, always a circus of hell and sweet and magic and silly disasters, and every story is a kind of repulsive magic story and always a musical about the most awful thing of all, life as disaster, such banal things, something like a fictional story about the sad life all around.

Once in Wadi Three, at the railroad station on the Damascus–Alexandria line, near the barrier on Herzl Street that would come down and divide the street, I saved a child whose name I no longer remember in the thorns under the train, after I saw a film at the Allenby movie house where somebody did that. I dreamed of saving somebody, never mind who, so they would admire my heroism and my concern, and I loved gigantic loves that started in the community center with Flash Gordon, the hero of our youth and savior of children.

On the seashore, our international hero, the hero of my generation, Simon Rudy acted and will continue acting today, as long as my generation lives. He came, I think, from Poland or Hungary, and was like a giant bulldog and would roar and the walls trembled from the hero who was Simon Rudy. How he appeared on the seashore on the boardwalk and wrapped himself in prayer shawls of iron with all his many goods and he would allow the tender women of Tel Aviv to feel his muscles and the chains they wrapped him in and would ask if somebody could imagine what a hero like him could do, and Tuvia the orphan, who came drunk every evening, would yell, "Sing!" And he got a smack that was still seen on his nose for several days and he roared with joy because Simon Rudy hit him and he came out alive and so did the hero, and Rudy made an effort, red as a tomato, his face twisted, his eyes shut with the effort, and the makeup on his eyelids ran yet stood in that wonderful encounter in the dark on the seashore near my sea garden lighted with beams of light from the headlights of the old

Harley Davidsons standing on both sides of the stage and illuminating it. And he would caper boldly, with eyes wide open and bulging muscles smeared with pure Shemen olive oil and the light turned them to furry gold, as in the Bible, and he would plug up the irons that flew in all directions and break silicon bricks with sharp blows and toss charming girls to the ceiling and catch them as they fell like feathers while breaking iron with his teeth.

What does Simon Rudy have to do with me? What did he have to do with my life in the hospital and with all the preparations to die with dignity? A nurse cleans my face. She has no connection with Simon Rudy, but maybe she's his daughter. Don't know if he had a daughter. She smiles gently, begs my pardon for the pain she's causing me. Day after day, as soon as I clear my throat they come to change the disgusting dressing, and at the side stands the doctor who checks the catheter, and Moishe Shabtai, who would stand next to Simon Rudy and was the best comb player in Tel Aviv, claims boldly that Smetana stole "Hatikva" from the Jews and wanted to be a war hero. Moishe Shabtai was such an ass, today he's called Max Levi. In 1949, we worked together on the sea, then I left and he stayed and worked as a stoker and sank with the *Bat Galim* in the Suez Canal and survived the Egyptian prison and beatings and tortures and went to America and married an ugly Jewish woman to get American citizenship and she brought a bakery as a dowry, and the champion comb player in the Middle East ended his life as a baker in Brooklyn. Moishe from the bakery in Brooklyn plays the comb and remembers that in the Simon Rudy club there was a beautiful Hungarian woman who would jump into a burning ring. There isn't one muscle in me that can be disguised as one of Simon Rudy's muscles, and I said then that Simon Rudy did that against everybody, a person dwelling alone in his muscles.

And as I hallucinate and know I'm hallucinating—and that's hard for me because I want to be existing and not just hallucinating, and not just hallucinatory—I dream and am not inventing things but living in dreams, I'm not proud or winning or losing. I can remember through the hallucinations that look true, but not without suspicion on my side, I can remember how the calm, warm Russian doctor who never loses human connection comes and wipes me because I am feverish and gives me an injection to bring down the fever and touches one of my hands, moves the stuck needle that hurts the back of my left hand and it's already filling with pus, and then he gives me another injection but in the stomach and I know that's the same injection as sixty years ago, when Agu's Topsy bit me on Arlozorov Street, and I try to touch the place where I was. Where I really was. This time it's so important for me to know what was really buried in the hallucinatory sketch. Why I was singing songs in my brain. How suddenly the

Russian songs of our youth choked me in the nonstop loop, "Sertsa," "Captain Captain Please Smile," "Tell Her Friends Why," and "Mix a Pear and an Apple," and where was I in the hallucinations? Is the secret of what is naïvely called "the war against cancer" buried in them?

I seek desperately the place where I don't know if I'm hallucinating or not. It's important for me today, more than all the fantasies I couldn't live without, to understand just one time. The second time you die, I imagine, there's nothing interesting. I also wonder what the meaning is of "he found his death," as the poet Ronny Someck said when an old Arab went swimming after curfew and was shot and they write in the newspapers that he "found his death." What is that? He went to look for his death and found it? And what is "the person passed away," and what is the "war against cancer?" Fear engenders a sickly grammar. You hear the words. They reek of the grave. There could also be the sense of revolt. What do you want from me? Why me of all people? Get off my back. Take somebody else. There are wicked people I can recommend.

Maybe I'll make myself an easy life when I call what was in me and everything where I stayed a long time: hell. And where do I get the right to talk about the suffering I suffered? Who hasn't suffered? Where do I get the right to measure my suffering by a yardstick against the suffering of someone who is starving to death in a camp, who is lying alive in a pile of dead people in the snow, in the frost near Tarnopol, my father's hometown, where his whole family was killed in a giant pit and shot and photographed as a souvenir. A woman once showed me a photo from Tarnopol where you see masses of people, and my family, too, standing in two lines and German soldiers are shooting them and in a little while they'll fall into the ditch they themselves dug before. And I recall our neighbor, Mr. Gelbard, who survived for years in Auschwitz. He was a cabinetmaker. He created charming wooden boxes for the Nazis to take home for the holidays, and they didn't want him to die, and he saw his children disappear. And once a year he would bring his friend to his house and make him sit under the table he had made of a special wood he found, and the man told him again and again how he sat with his baby in his arms under the bridge, how there were dozens of fugitives from the ghetto with him, how Germans came to the bridge and sat down to rest and how the baby started shrieking and how everybody looked at him with sad and supplicating looks with extinguished eyes and how he choked the baby with his own hands. So who am I and what is my suffering compared to that man?

I always do that to myself. Try to put things in perspective, and the truth is that we're all grasshoppers and I'm one grasshopper among them and a leech of a person and I'm really small and unimportant. And the cancer is a maestro and multifaceted, and there are those who die immediately and those who don't die immediately. Cancer's not just a happening, not a birthday, even though it belongs to something that takes place in the domain of time. It's something that rises up to kill you, lies in ambush, reveals itself, and then strikes.

Suddenly they bring some expert to examine me. A nurse gives me a sponge bath. They try to teach me to lift a hand. I lie and look at a nurse, she says, "Hug me and that's how you can move." I feel bad, I'm ashamed and refuse, and she says, "Yoram, don't treat me as a woman, I'm here to take care of you, hold me tight, hug me very hard, because you have to learn to stand up," and I'm an offended fool, I want to explain to her that a woman is always a woman, and I look at the Palestinian pigeon from the Nakba on the windowsill and the only thing I can see aside from this fucking room is the window, and the outside in the window, and the lights go out slowly in the evening and come on at dawn in the window, and they look at the world, at the city and the streets that I'm a stranger to, I'm finished now, and the Palestinian pigeon craps and the sensitive nurse, she seems to be blushing, and if I had arms I would hold them out and hug her. For me a nurse is a woman, and she doesn't want me to know her as a woman.

She's thirty-eight years old, she told me, and like most of the nurses, she came from Russia. Her husband wasn't Jewish, and he fled back to Russia with her money as soon as he didn't need her Jewishness anymore. Every day she cleaned her small apartment and worked in a needle factory, and one day she knelt down to clean a spot on the floor and a cockroach got into her mouth. She was scared and tried to spit it out, but the cockroach didn't want to leave. She became hysterical, picked up a fork and stuck it in her mouth to get the cockroach out, and in her panic, she swallowed the fork. They took her to the hospital here downstairs and took out the fork, but the cockroach wasn't found. She saw the x-rays of the fork in her stomach and took them home and hung them in her small living room, and instead of watching television, she'd sit at the x-rays and laugh. They did a story about her in the weekend supplement. They put it on some website. A man came from America and said that on the Internet he saw an article about her and the cockroach she swallowed and the fork, and he decided to be an artist and make an exhibition of her x-rays. His charming idiocy pleased her and he cut and arranged the x-rays of the fork and said it was original and idiotic and so museums all over the world would buy it. The director of the Tel Aviv Museum lavished praise on it, and the man took her shoe and licked the inside of it and said he was crazy about women's shoes and when he was sufficiently aroused he came on top of her and she felt in his mouth the smell of her feet and for the first time in her life she understood what bliss is. That's what she said. The exhibition was a great success and the newspaper *Haaretz* wrote that it emphasized mass villainy and the equator of the atlas and the future. They bought an apartment on Bloch Street, and her ex-husband came from White Russia because he smelled money. She divorced him, and was pleased with her man's love of shoes, and she bought about ten pairs of shoes and put them on and he licked all of them and went into the neighbors' apartments and stole shoes and in the building they said somebody was stealing women's shoes, but as one of the neighbor women told the TV correspondent he really didn't look like somebody who steals women's shoes, as if there is somebody who does look like somebody who steals women's shoes. In the end, he dropped dead of excitement and she adopted a dog, named the dog after him, and came to work in the hospital, rich as she was, because even without pay she loved to see patients and to help them.

I open my eyes. Find myself taking a small elephant, or more precisely, a shrunken elephant, for a walk on Dizengoff Street when it was still sandy and they were about to pave it, and big potbellied landlords bought and sold the buildings on the street, some of them not yet built. Then I wake up, what was that? What's happening to me all the time? LSD is child's play compared to the drugs I live on and that keep my suffering at bay. I leave the hospital and go to the seashore near the old Sheraton that hasn't been there for a long time because the fools destroyed it and I take pleasant walks there so I can fall asleep. I look at the ceiling. The Palestinian pigeons from the Nakba flew off on a sortie to Mecca, marking a way for the sword, and then they circled in the air and came back.

Far away downstairs, at the entrance to the hospital, I hear sirens of ambulances arriving at the emergency room. A pain grows sharp when there is no possibility of remembering it. You can remember that it was a pain, but not what it was or how it was. Damn it, you can't remember the pain itself. Maybe it is that the wisdom of the body close to death is to forget suffering. I console myself with Lessing's article about not everybody who mocks chains being free of them. But I didn't really mock. Ultimately, I was bound in handcuffs. To communicate I had to move my weary hands. They had to guess what I wanted. I was a body swollen with fluids and full of spaces running wild and I tried to point to the small board with the letters but my hands were weak and I couldn't.


One night I feel bad, it is dark, I manage to find the call button and I ring. A tall Russian nurse comes. He moves like a bat. He stands in front of me and looks as if he wants to understand what I want. He tries to guess words in Hebrew and I look at him and wonder why I'm torturing him. He tells me he had little children in Rishon LeZion, that his wife got sick, that his mother was coming from Russia in two days, and he stands before me like a giant question mark, almost transparent, all the troubles of life on him, he's got difficult patients here and he's tired and he's trying to figure out what I want and it's hard for him. I look at him and see deep hatred for me, I'm getting on his nerves, I want to console him and can't, I gesture to him to go, he wonders what to do; in the end, he comes very, very close to my body, sad, full of regret, and makes an opening in my chest, moves the lid over the connection to the tubing, and says, "Speak," and I bring up from the abyss of the body a few words from the edge of my body, "I want," and he understands and does what I want and blocks the opening and from then until my last day in isolation, I don't see him again.

Because my brain would get into breaks of death and I could also usually hear a lot, I flew between worlds, committed myself—or at least that's how I remember it today but I don't remember to whom—to remembering a happy day in my life, to sustain the disappointment that a chapter had ended, that I was on my way out, another month, another year, that's it. But I'm not dead. I finished dying. I start living. Not such a big deal. Maybe that was the idea of one of the doctors, who saw that the football games on the screen moving all the time without sound didn't change a thing in me and I really didn't see them, they were like a visual wallpaper, and he decided I had to live again in a beautiful moment that really existed, maybe had to know, to be sure I once had a life. I thought of something I could think about from every point in time. That day was somehow like the heart of the amusements of my soul. I was in my hallucination and couldn't give it up. I was once a young man and it's pouring rain and I'm walking in the Jezreel Valley from the highway toward Kibbutz Beit Alpha. The Mountains of Gelboa before me are covered with what is called "thick clouds" but is apparently a mistake and should be "darkness." "Mass" appears only once in the Bible but it's a nicer word than it sounds, and there is fog and the rain falls on me more than it comes down and embraces me. I feel good to be part of the heavy rain, with my feet sinking in the mud. Nobody is with me. After some time the rain stops and a rainbow goes through the sky and wind blows and I am tired. I lie down in the wet field, in the mud, near me narcissi are blooming and buttercups and red and blue anemone, the air touches me and the fragrance of wet grass comes to my nose. The ground is comfortable, I look at the clouds and I see them shape themselves, and I love the sight from below and I lie supine.

And here I was in bed and I don't know how; I came out of the valley, it was a dream, and tears filled my eyes and I don't know why, and I was about to come back to what had always seemed so obvious to me. I don't really remember what happened, what I do remember is that there was a hitch, they had to dig another opening in my throat or my chest and only afterward did they discover that I was responding again. I felt sticky and heavy and not unpleasant, like a kind of thick soup, and I love thick soups, but to eat them, not to be cast in them. I wanted to go back to something right, something resistant in the teeth of time. People wrote books about how they came back from death. They described lights. A tunnel. Flashes. All their life passes before their eyes. Nonsense. There's only one death, even though the dead are different from one another. And if there's only one death, then the death people love to describe is nothing but imagination or a lie. There's nothing real in the nothing. Death isn't something concrete but the end of the working of the brain. For two or three weeks I was at that end. There was nothing there. Only mud.

I sank in the mud as I did back then sixty-five years ago in the valley on the way to Beit Alfa, and I recalled hitchhiking back to Tel Aviv, to my sea, and I saw the window and flew through it to north Tel Aviv and was amazed at that journey, almost Yotam the magician, and I was with Max the Lunatic, another one of my childhood heroes, near the Model School where Sara my mother taught and where my sister studied and Rina and Sarah and Mina and Amos and Amihud and

Shalom and Hannah Ehrenkranz and Shlomit and Zilpha S. with the bra and Ora Becker and Abigail Soroka and Nahman and Nahum Shomroni and I and everybody else, and I sat on the hills with Max the Lunatic who wore felt slippers and stuck weathervanes on the roof of his hut and really loved only what crawled or swam in the sea, and said we were lucky we were once fish, and he saw gills in me and a fish sired me, not Moshe my father but a fish, and then, as every day, he repeated the joke about the German Jew who had three dogs and called them to come, and one came and one didn't come, and one came or didn't. He would say that only the sea was the *heimat*—the homeland, the home, the place in the deep sense, a word with no equal in describing a place of belonging in any other language except German— the real homeland of the Jews, because they didn't work it, but in fact he aimed his words at Teacher Vitkin, who, every night, read his son Tel Hai stories of Jewish heroes from the book *Memories of the House of David*, published by Jezreel in a blue binding, and stories of the Shomer and stories of "Nili" by Ya'ari Polskin, and the Book of the Haganah and stories of building the Land and the Hebrew Brigade.

Tel Hai Vitkin would listen in panic, and even Teacher Gedalia ben-Horin thought that Teacher Vitkin went too far, even though he loved him dearly. They lived next door to one another on Yoash Street for forty years, their houses lapped by the sea near the deserted port of Tel Aviv, and

Teacher Gedalia ben-Horin didn't forgive Teacher Vitkin as he didn't forgive Dzuash for the lectures he gave us about the Hebrew army we would be; he died of a heart attack in the Italian air raid on Tel Aviv, and he didn't forgive Vitkin for yelling about the Jews who didn't fight to the death in the Holocaust and went like sheep to the slaughter. "Here, we're different!" yelled Vitkin. "We'll win! We'd have beaten the Germans, too!" And we felt affection mixed with scorn for those two old men, how modesty and honesty throbbed in them both and we never managed to decide which one we'd rather join to establish the Hebrew army or the Hebrew state, Teacher Vitkin or Gedalia ben-Horin.

We would march in perfect order along the Yarkon River and hit one another with bulrushes to train for the future war with the British foe and to learn stratagems and war tactics. And Mrs. Leipzig from the corner grocery, who hated Vitkin even more than she hated Gedalia ben-Horin, said that no army, Hebrew or not, would get out of here, here there are jackals, because she heard the jackals at night, and from the hills she heard and my mother Sarah also heard the song "There Are Foxes There," and my mother Sara, "How beautiful are the jackals in Canaan, like the nights that were chill and clear they are, and the desolation..." And the jackals came, and Mrs. Leipzig was afraid of them and said that only Nazis would come and no Arabs, because Arabs were afraid of the Debbas called hyenas, and the Haganah had a lot of Debbas in secret breeding farms in the kibbutzim and she said that the two of them, Teacher Vitkin and Teacher Gedalia ben-Horin, were bad because they were Zionists and because of them she had to flee from cultured Germany to Palestine with the falafel and the sabras.

And out of great hostility to his wife, Teacher Vitkin started smearing mustard on his ear so his wife would bite it and learn a lesson because she was Mapai and he was Faction B, and out of habit he started chewing on pencils that became an occupation he fostered also against Albion—that is, Great Britain, which he wanted to shrink. He had a collection of hundreds of pencils to chew on and wanted to contribute them to science or to the Haganah but he admitted to us that neither wanted them. His request was accompanied by an emotional letter asking them to invent a salve against the British, but he didn't know what ancient or modern Hebrew science needed chewed pencils. He was so fanatical for the impending Zionist revolution that he stopped tarring the roof on nearby Yordei Sirah Street because he saw a *HaMishmar* newspaper on the mat at the entrance to the house, and the comrades in their movement would constantly yell, "Strong" and "Strong and Bold."

Vitkin was deeply offended when the gossips acting on behalf of Mrs. Leipzig said that when he, Vitkin, came out of the house without a coat and in sandals like King David, even on rainy days, his dear son Tel Hai, the future hero of

Israel's victory, took that opportunity to close the windows and wrap himself up, goodness gracious, in a blanket, and finally he went out wearing, yes, wearing a sweater, a real sweater, like some Diaspora Jew. Poor Teacher Vitkin heard and wept, "My dear son won't be bar Kokhba. He wears a sweater," and they told him that bar Kokhba himself must have worn a sweater in winter because great warriors can feel cold and heat whenever they want, but he wouldn't hear of it. And now he saw chewing pencils as some victory over the decadent Diaspora, when people bought what he called "all nonsense," and Tel Hai his son took revenge on Teacher Gedalia when he got Mrs. Leipzig to spread a rumor that Gedalia played the piano with his feet while sitting on a chair.

Vitkin's landlord was the doctor of philosophy Zalman Zelikovitch, and Zalman Zelikovitch's wife had disappeared years ago, and those who knew or didn't know said she had run away with a handsome blond Polish officer from Anders' Army who was then in the Land of Israel. Zelikovitch also had a beautiful daughter. One day Vitkin fainted on Mughrabi Street when his dear son's glasses fell off while they were making a giant human pyramid in the shape of a Star of David, on which Tel Hai, the most nimble and slippery of them all, formed the apex. And as he tried to catch his glasses, the whole pyramid collapsed, a symbol of the rebirth of the Hebrew nation in its own land. What intensified the pain and the ideological oppression was the fact that Mrs. Leipzig discovered that Tel Hai Vitkin was in love with Zelikovitch's daughter, and she wasn't ashamed to go to the great enemy, the Zionist Vitkin, and denounce his son, because she loved to hate more than to love.

Stunned, Vitkin sat his son down and delivered a three-hour speech on Zionism, on self-denial as the way to national resurrection, on sublimation, on the proper love for the Israeli person, on the stratagems of war and the victory of the socialist Jewish person over nature, and then Zelikovitch's beautiful daughter passed by, and Zelikovitch, who became a right-wing Revisionist in old age, threw the newspaper *HaMishmar* at two Arabs passing on the way to the British army camp, where the Hilton Hotel is today, and his daughter passed by them and went into a wind blowing from the sea and her skirt rose, and Tel Hai, struck by her beauty, got up as if he were running amok and ran out to her, and Teacher Vitkin looked like the statue of an ancient, pained prince, and Zelikovitch's daughter took Tel Hai to the Metzudat Ze'ev building, where he did military drills in brown uniforms like the Italians, in a fort that was only partially built back then, and he started wearing a brown belt diagonally across his chest and talking about gladiators and the kingdom of Israel, and Mrs. Leipzig said, "He's got charm, goyish charm," and we told her Zelikovitch wasn't a goy, but she insisted that if he wasn't a goy he should be, and she said, "And how, he's a goy," and we saw a smile glowing on Leipzig's face for the first time since she came from Germany, even ben-Horin said afterward, "Really, the first since she got off the ship in the port of Tel Aviv, when we came to sing 'The wheels of the world are squeaky in the works' to the poor immigrants and they stood in their suits and looked at us and thought they had arrived in Africa." And Mrs. Leipzig smiled and said, "Why, what, didn't I see? Once he did that, you know, in the sand near my store, did it, you know what, watered a garden without a hose, au naturel, and I saw and I say to you, child, there aren't any Jews like that."

Miranda isn't here yet, neither is Naomi, and Zelikovitch's daughter yells, "You're all converts in spirit, crippled hearts," and what will I tell her? I plead with her to leave me and understand that here I'm on a breathing machine, I'm in Ichilov, on the rivers of Babylon or the rivers of the Dnieper, with no character, they do with me what they want, wipe, stretch on the side of the bed, and all of a sudden I'm also a goy, why not, I'll raise an army for the war against doctors. "And you," said Zelikovitch's nationalist daughter, "you won't be the descendants of the Maccabees no matter how you spell it and you won't be heroes the Diaspora Jews were scared of and took out of the Bible, leaving only the lamentations and the grief. And if you call me goy once more, I'll leave you and denounce you to Etzel, who will finish you off."

The whole issue of denunciation started after Max the Lunatic said that Teacher Vitkin saved an Arab in the riots of 1936 and hid him on the roof, while Gedalia ben-Horin besieged the house to take the Arab prisoner. Vitkin defended the Arab with a Turkish carbine he found in the attic and afterward they called him "Arab on the roof," because apparently it was hard to call him "Vitkin who hid an Arab on the roof," and Vitkin didn't give in, even to Mrs. Leipzig, who barely knew a hundred words in Hebrew and wanted to turn him over to the Haganah. The proud Hebrew teacher Gedalia, who taught me Mishnah, helped Max the Lunatic and didn't tease us for our friendship with him, didn't scold us for the food we'd bring him, and taught us to measure wind and distance and temperatures and guess whether rain would fall, in the words of Teacher Gedalia, who didn't like the weak prophets and yelled, "Never will a lion live with a lamb."

Teacher Gedalia ben-Horin said the denouncer Mrs. Leipzig said Max the Lunatic had been a veterinarian in Leipzig in Germany, to which Mrs. Leipzig added the epithet "damned" and spoke evil about it in broken Hebrew after she learned some disconnected words. And Teacher Gedalia ben-Horin said Max knew if it would rain or not. And those are my days, hollow, unclear. Were Vitkin and ben-Horin a hallucination, as nurse Natasha says? And the people who come and go before me, who are they? In the hospital, they're like turgid water. The isolation room is separated and sterile and maybe stinking, although because of the respirator I don't smell anything. Apparently it was comfortable for me to go back to some part of my childhood, back then, when I was still alive. When I had a future. The memories and hallucinations blended more and more with a completely unnecessary reality. In the hospital it's hot or cold, I can't remember. Blood flows from my nose, I weep without knowing why or wherefore. I think if it was true that Miranda saved me from death, it's a sign it was worth it.

I tell her, Miranda, sweetheart, darling, apple of my eye, you once asked me why the Jews pour their wrath on the goyim and I explained to you that "mother-in-law" in Hebrew means "wrath," not "warmth," and it says "pour your wrath on the goyim," and not "your warmth on the goyim," and in our family I'm a Jewish minority, in the Ministry of the Interior our daughters are called by the name of a new and unknown nationality called "American," something between Brazil and South Dakota apparently, and you shouldn't have prevented me from going and dying. And why is it really so important to know if that was all true or not? Why does truth always have to be so holy? Is there truth at all? If I think I saw, I saw.

Today, looking back after coming back, I'm aware that all this sounds untenable. I'm home now. I'm Yoram snatched from the fire in Israel, an expression the old Hasid who lived across from us liked to use. He's fond of me. Or I dreamed it.

pool and Ricardo Montalbán, the slick shmuck, sang to her, and the pool was illuminated with thousands of lights, but that happened in fact during the war, in 1948, when we went to see the only film to be seen in the bombarded city, and hallucinations aren't dreams. Estherke jumps into the water, seventy virgins in bathing suits surround Estherke as she swims on her back and I feel a strong need to explain that I also fell victim.

So I tried to locate myself in the slow progress in my recovery, if I am indeed recovering. The diseases depend on us. Afterward, they'll seek metastases and there will be other difficult tests and I'll know if I've recovered completely. And what is completely? For how long is completely? And all that with the assumption that life truly has meaning, as if all those who talk about "finding yourself" and "how to be yourself" and "how to realize yourself," as if all those aren't only vanity and a striving after wind. What meaning can life have? Death is waiting for every living thing. And what is the meaning of "soul," what is a "soul"? In the Bible, there is no soul. Proper Jews don't have a soul. They're not concerned with it. Only afterward in the Talmud did the soul begin to play such an important part. Then they started burying corpses. In a few years six million people living in Israel today will have to die, where will there be room to bury them? And what is the meaning of life everybody talks about? Life expectancy today is about eighty years. A third of those eighty years we're sleeping, we miss the first years because it's impossible to really remember them, the last ones because of diseases and forgetting, and the years we waste waiting for a green light or for the phone to connect or the computer to boot up or hot water to flow after cold, and three or four years we spend in the toilet—there's no meaning, life is like a belch, a kind of process that isn't serious, we're like seaweed, neither of us has a reason to live except to increase and bring into the world other creatures who have no reason to exist, and what is the meaning of a mountain or a rock? The compulsive need of human beings to find meaning is very disappointing. If life had sense and there was meaning, they would be written in our genetic code.

Suddenly I am no longer a question mark in my empty head, with momentary flickers of memories and evasive dreams, but a person assumed to be working. And I stink, and look like a bull swollen with hot air, I'm a giant wheel. Did the cancer truly enter me on purpose? Was I truly walking on Eduard Bernstein Street and it came into me of all people and then of all times? How can there be meaning to life when you know that you die into nothing? And if you die without life after death, there's no meaning to a search for meaning. That cancer and my cancer, they're also random.

But then I was in another place, I was driving my poor Peugeot and the car, as usual, broke down, and I was riding on a bike I had when I was young and I came to the department store and sat down above a giant hall, in Hamburg apparently, a giant department store, tens of thousands of people walking around like junkies and buying whatever they can put their hands on. I found myself sitting in a giant chandelier of colored glass, like a kaleidoscope. Twenty or thirty yards in diameter, an enormous Tiffany lamp, all of it pieces of glass in various colors. I don't remember how long I sat among slivers of glass and how I arrived and where I arose, but I knew I was seen because I myself saw me. Below, about twenty stories under me, I saw the Swiss minister of defense, and I don't know how but I do know it was he, and I thought I also saw the plump Swiss soldier wearing a spotted uniform, whom I had seen waddling in the Zurich railroad station, and I wrote a poem about him, "Where are you running, Swiss soldier? What is threatening you, Swiss soldier?" And I saw Hamutal Ansky walking around downstairs with a group of people and I didn't know any of them except the minister of defense. She saw me and was angry. She yelled at me to come down. I yelled back that I couldn't, that I was locked in a glorious Tiffany chandelier or maybe now it was a crystal chandelier, and I couldn't move, the truth is I also knew I didn't want to, I really and truly had no desire to come down, even though sitting wasn't comfortable and I was swinging and almost fell. Hamutal Ansky called to me again to come, she said she'd brought a group of journalists from France who wanted to interview me and know why, making movements of speaking but she threw up her hands and said, "Sorry, I'm busy and don't have time now to guess you," and then I recalled I had once heard that there was a sign on the door of the Reform synagogue in Houston, Texas, that said, "Closed for the Jewish holidays." Nurse Regina came and gave me an injection, and I wanted to ask her what her compulsive need was to prick me all the time, and I looked a little at the football players who were arguing with somebody who was probably the referee, and I asked the nurse if she had seen Hamutal Ansky, but I didn't have a voice and she shrugged and I lay in bed on the inflated rubber mattress my wonderful Naomi bought for me when I came to the ward, and I was indifferent.

Sarah from Café Tamar told me afterward, I mean months afterward, when I visited her in the café, that I didn't die because they didn't want me there. And Sarah has influence over all of us, and probably over death. She distributes slices of garlic to her lovers and saves them. She also knows everybody who died, and I believe what she says. I would come to her in the café just to make sure I was alive, because she knows about the dead before they do.


Somebody came to the hospital and called me Lazarus. I saw before my eyes an ancient landscape. Land of the fathers. A monk in a brown robe came to visit. I asked him if Lazarus truly came back from the dead like me, and he said there were three witnesses with him, Mary Magdalene and her sister Martha, and I asked who else and he said, "God, of course," and smiled. I seemed in fact to be lying in bed and hallucinating, and then I knew I was hallucinating, and the truth was that it felt good to hallucinate because I was afraid to live again, death was comfortable, the return was insipid, unnecessary, I was afraid of getting back to life, of worrying about the rent, buying new trousers, calling my sister to ask how she was, contributing money to telephone solicitors. Here there is no phone, Miranda answers the phone, I have no need to talk, to justify myself, I'm fatally ill and I'm allowed to do anything, what will I do if I truly come back?

The monk who came to visit me in the hospital sat next to me and I started talking with him because so far he'd been silent. He said he came from Germany but spoke fluent Hebrew, and he said, "You talk about Saint Augustine and Jerome and how Lazarus came back from death," and I asked him how he knew that I talked about Jerome and Augustine, and he answered that he had read my books with quotations from Jerome and also "yearning for Christianity and love and hate for Christianity," and he said it's now 1967, "and you occupied and liberated and annexed," and I was amazed at how it could be 1967, and he looked angry and said, "The Talmud is a book of barren arguments about irrelevant matters. It's religion without an ethos, without dogma, without a myth, without glory, without cathedrals, without mystery, without God, without music, without ceremony, without ritual, without beautiful painting, without Satan, with angels who are only messengers, without hell in heaven, without sin as painful as eternal sin, a religion that praises chattering, that teaches children ways of excommunicating woman, that teaches legal killing, that teaches that it's permitted to kill mercilessly everyone God orders killed, a religion like that isn't a religion, it's rubbish. And what's even more awful, you don't have spiritual fathers, even your Messiah can't really come, your Messiah is ultimately yearnings, because you didn't believe the Messiah who came and who was called Christ." And I told him that that's what I love about us even though I'm far from being religious, and he got mad and said, "Religion without miracles is like a letter without a signature."

"In Judaism, which isn't really religion," I told him, "very few miracles happened for three thousand years, the walls of Jericho and the container of oil and Moses's water from the rock, so the Jewish frequency of miracles is quite limited, and so there's nothing really to wait for, and religion is a mystery," and I told the monk that Dostoevsky wrote that Christianity is the miracle, the mystery, and the authority, and he said, "Christianity isn't a vague muttering of prayers and concern with urine, castration, contempt for women, nakedness. And your children have to memorize when a woman is fit for intercourse. Where do you have mercy and glory and where do you have saints?"

I waited for him to finish because I didn't want to offend him, I didn't want him to think I wasn't polite because I was an occupier, and I hurried to go with him to a small camp on top of the mountain to appease the soldiers or maybe they were the youth corps, poor sons of occupiers, or go know who today. I spoke of our pure righteousness, of Jewish fate, of no choice, of rising and coming, of brothers sitting and "friends" as a mystical song that doesn't exist in our reality, and about a nation that doesn't give up excavations of its life, and about happy is he who dies with Tel Hai as his leader, and about the power of the brain and the brain of the power, and about when thou wast in thy blood Live, and about a land of desert and glory, and about God from the mountains, and about paratroopers weeping at the Western Wall, and he heard, he smiled and he was silent, and before we parted, he said, "The occupier will choke on his occupation." Did that happen? Maybe I'm coming back very slowly to some sanity.

The doctors decrease the dose of drugs. They take me as a drunk and within a few days I finally have to come back to sanity, but in stages, very slowly, and so I live in constant fear of what I remember, if it was or wasn't, and of my life in the world of black-and-white. The blood-pressure meter still feeds the monitor and my dear ones are at the edge of nothingness and I hear voices that sound as if they really want me to come back. Naomi my daughter looks at me. I want to kiss her because she brings me love but I don't have real and true lips to kiss her.

Four months later, in our house on Bilu Street, where I'm now lying in bed, it's the end of August and I'm free of hallucinations, of the hospital, and of the illness, and I move a little, and am ugly and old. I didn't have the courage to jump out the window in the hospital, and the apartment is on the ground floor and there are bars, and Miranda, the apple of my eye, my darling, next to me in bed, puts a diaper on me. I notice that something is missing, I look in panic at the belly and don't find the belly button that had been there for seventy-five years and I ask, "What happened to my belly button?" And Miranda looks with a smile and she doesn't find it either and I call Jay on the cell phone and tell him I lost my belly button and he says, "Look on the side of the belly," and I and Miranda look on the side of the belly and he says, "See, there's a little pleat," and I look and see that there really is a miserable little pleat, and Jay says to me, "Note, in the pleat there's a notch," and I look and admit and am comforted: I see a small notch that was once my beautiful belly button. "Find it?" he asks. "What did those surgeons have against my belly button?" I ask. "Why did the bastards move it?"

Everything looked like a cosmic exercise against me because I lay here alive and couldn't die. Here, look at me in my shame, daughters of Jerusalem. I've fallen alive like those who fell in Pompeii, and after they were filled with plaster, they looked like the human beings they had been before they were devoured, and I looked at them and thought that Lazarus, with whom I was compared, would have said they didn't understand him. That he really didn't want John the Baptist's Martha and Mary's sister and Mary, the sister of Jesus, to see him when he was abandoned to death and woke up from the tomb. I would have told him he didn't know it but he lived in a world that isn't anymore. And I wanted to ask him the meaning of the chapter "from dust you came and to dust you shall return." I wasn't born of dust, I was born of millions of years of prehuman and then human evolution, I'm the end of hundreds of millions of years of existence and the end of my parents and my parents' parents. I came from distant grandfathers, from ancient generations, from Sabbateans in Ukraine and Frankists in Tarnopol, from one who was Rabbi Akiva and from Simeon bar Yochai, and like every one of us I was born from the vicissitudes of historical longevity, because in our loins we complete the circle we are destined to complete because we are destined not to be born but to die. All of us ultimately are edges of people.

All of us are the completion of a season of life. In my life I gave life to my daughters so they would die without being connected to the sins of their father. Doesn't God say to Cain, "and if thou doest not well, sin lieth at the door. And unto thee shall be his desire and thou shalt rule over him"? And I thought the desire for sin is the drug of life. "Thou hast sinned" is a light to us. At our door it lies. We lust for it. But do we really have to rule over it?

I talk with Sarah my mother. Miranda says I abandoned Sarah while she was alive, that I mistreated her. That I made her cry. I didn't know how to love her, and then she got old and I was bad to her and she was good to me. Now I lie and try to restore Sarah my mother. Suddenly I miss her. I exploited her, and damaged her good name. I didn't pity her. I didn't know how to love her. Every morning, Sarah my mother would do her hair and go to the clinic in old Ramat Aviv and sit and wait a long time without complaining and without pushing, and was examined. And that's how they'd kill cancers when they were still small. The doctors died of old age and diseases, but others came and the clerks were also replaced, only she remained every day, except the Sabbath, and would sit and wait for examinations. And would triumph over all the cancers but she remained so alone since Moshe my father died on her, because in my family you don't die, you die on others, as a kind of revenge. "If you drown," my mother would yell on the seashore, "I'll

187

kill you." And Moshe my father left her with his death and that was a kind of infidelity to her from him, and I also left, and my sister Mira left to live her life.

Basically, it's good to die to prevent suicide.

I don't like deformations. It's hard for me to look at myself now. All my life I've served beauty. I love beautiful people. I don't live well with hunchbacks, ugly women, and, like Moses our Teacher, I don't like what looks too ugly to stand in the Tabernacle, so they said no to the lame, no to scabies, no to leprosy, no to blindness—those poor wretches won't get to see God, but if there's something in the body that can't be seen, cancer for example, oh, that's all right. But what's strange is that if something looks ugly and perverse, like leprosy, why is it bad in the eyes of the Hebrews, who determined and didn't really follow "Favor is deceitful and beauty is vain" and "Don't look at the jar but what is in it"? We didn't make beautiful jars here. If the Tabernacle really looked like research suggests it did when it was restored, there'd be no reason to look at it.

When you're sick everybody runs away from you, there is no greatness in us, no aesthetic, we're old, take up space, empty the state treasury with our sickness and have no reason to live, we're idiots who cling to life and have no grief for ourselves, but only self-pity. Self-pity is bad for the soul. And the basis of aesthetics is that it has no God.

*

In the end, I came back to life. One day, a procession of doctors came. They examined me. They didn't look at me. They read the charts written by the night nurses, hanging as usual on the bed. Suddenly one of them said, "That's it, got to go forward. We'll take out the catheter and the feeding tube, but you'll have to sit in a chair they'll bring here, and we'll see." Everything happened very fast. Taking out the feeding tube was painful, but it was great to be free after two months. I found the voice that had abandoned me and I started saying a few words. Miranda came to learn my voice and seemed amazed, as if she had forgotten how it sounded, and Naomi came and nurses came to congratulate me, and then they ordered me not to drink until the sores healed. They let me lick cotton dipped in water, but I couldn't drink, and liquids no longer flowed from the feeding tube and I dried out. That was a Calvary. I pleaded with them to let me drink. They explained to me that I couldn't yet. I was willing to donate my heart to Jay Lavie's transplant department in Tel Hashomer if they gave me even one glass of water for it. A whole heart for one glass of water!

Licking cotton dipped in water didn't help, and I imagined I was sitting in a cart full of locked bottles of water, I tried to open them with my teeth, and meanwhile orderlies came and put me into a blanket. By now I weighed as much as a small child, the puffiness of my body, which had looked so ugly for months, was beginning to vanish—I lost maybe fifty pounds—and they put me in an easy chair and I was asked to sit in it for a whole hour. I didn't enjoy it. They wanted the body to get a bit round, my muscles to start working. After three months of lying, sitting was bad and hard. A swarthy, vigorous girl came and started working with me and made me raise my fingers a little. She asked me to want more and to be a little more generous and ambitious, and I tried, the word "ambitious" worked on me, and a few days later I managed to lift a finger for a moment and make a few movements and today I don't remember what they were, and then it was decided to let me drink. I wanted to drink as much as possible but I couldn't swallow and almost choked.

They told me it had been decided to take me off the respirator. They examined everything that had to be examined and warned me that it would be hard, that it took a lot of time to take some patients off the respirator and that at Tel Hashomer there was even a course for weaning from the respirator, since confidence in breathing is crucial. They told me not to despair. That was a moment of vague dread, and suddenly I felt alone in the world without the respirator that had been like a mother to me. I was a three-month-old baby and they cut me off from my mother's breast. I sat in bed, leaning on the pillows and for the first time in months I breathed real air. The window next to me was open. Outside it was blazing summer. A thin wind blew inside and I filled my lungs with air and I was dizzy and my eyes were laughing, and I felt it in the roots of my hair and I was like a drunk and I smiled. They stood above me and said they had never seen a real smile on my face, a smile of someone who came out of the garbage, and now they saw and admitted to me that that was ideal, a gift, and some nurse said, "Look, we finally did good work here!" It felt good to breathe. The lungs filled with air and the fog that flowed from the machine no longer hummed in my ear. Today it's hard to remember exactly what the feeling was. It seemed to liberate in me a shame about myself. For what a weakling I was. I don't like wine, and when I was a drinker I'd drink whiskey or brandy or vodka or beer, not wine, but the feeling was what many people attribute to wine. After half an hour, I was choking a little and they connected me to the machine again. First they put an oxygen mask on my face. Instead of weeks, within three days, I was breathing on my own.

I had a new series of tests, and now I was fed up with the place. Everything looked disgusting. I'm breathing, get me out of here. I'm alive. They found a rehabilitation center for me at Tel Hashomer, and by now I was helpless and fed up and wanted to go through what was fastest, and one of the doctors said I needed to start eating real food and should start with something light, porridge, for example. I said, "Anything but porridge." I saw the porridge in the hospital. It looked like something that isn't, as the farmer said when they took him to the zoo and showed him a giraffe and he said,

"There is no such thing!" And I asked if mashed potatoes would be all right. The doctor said they certainly would. I was longing for mashed potatoes and scrambled eggs, but in the hospital you don't get scrambled eggs or soft-boiled eggs, only rubbery fried eggs. And then they brought me a plate of mashed potatoes from the kitchen. I tasted a first spoonful of mashed potatoes and I felt as if a new tube had been put into me and I wanted to throw up. The taste was disgusting, because I hadn't eaten for so long, but also because only in hospitals is mashed potatoes a perfect example of how not to cook, which should be a required course in every university. I sat facing the nurse who was feeding me and I wanted so much to eat something that wasn't mashed potatoes. A day or two later, the doctor on duty said that if I didn't eat something, they'd have to put the damn feeding tube back in me, and I couldn't bear that. Miranda said she thought I might like ice cream. She hurried downstairs, bought ice cream, brought it up, and fed it to me with a big spoon and suddenly I could eat. I didn't taste the ice cream but it felt nice in my throat.

For a few days, I lived almost only on ice cream and yogurt mixed with powdered egg white, minerals, and vitamins, and then they told me, Yoram, in a few days you're leaving. For the first time since I was hospitalized, I protested against the hospital. Suddenly I hated it. They knew I had recovered, that I hated the doctors, the nurses. I shook, raised my voice, and yelled. I yelled that I was fed up with them. That I wanted to get out of here and couldn't be here anymore. I was willing to take a risk. The professor himself came to see me. He said it would be arranged. He told me how I was dying and all that, I waited, I was nervous, it was hard for me to talk with the nurses or the doctors, they had to sew up some openings in my chest and my throat that hadn't yet healed, I ate yogurt and ice cream and the holes healed, and in the morning smiling doctors came and wished me luck. Nurses came, and Miranda and Naomi and Mira and Jay, and the orderlies took me down in a gurney and the family took my rubber mattress and the rest of my things downstairs. An ambulance was waiting, I was laid in it, the door was closed, Miranda sat next to me, the driver said something I didn't hear and I saw a male nurse weeping in the door of the hospital and that touched me. Suddenly I was alive, feeling the earth move beneath me. Looking out the window of the ambulance and seeing Tel Aviv not through shutters from the depths of reality, and seeing everything upside down. I saw trees with enormous red blossoms and didn't understand exactly where I was.

A while later, we came to Tel Hashomer. We went through the depths of the gigantic hospital and as I still lay supine, I saw a hotel and a shopping center and we came to the rehabilitation center near the Bakum Fence. Now we were traveling in a Land of Israel that hadn't been for some time, among thick cypresses, eucalyptuses, gigantic treetops, tree trunks hundreds of years old, prickly-pear hedges, bluish vines and gigantic bougainvillea, purple and ardent, climbing vines and wildflowers, and I wanted to hug a tree, kiss wild branches, and we came to the center, a pleasant place that looked like a small kibbutz. They took down the gurney, wheeled me inside, to the air-conditioned lobby, and I lay on the gurney. They driver left us and said he had a "passed-away person" to take to the Burial Society, and I said, "What, they come and they go?!" He gave me a mischievous look and said, "It could have been the other way around."

I thought to myself, fifty-eight years ago I came back from the war shrouded in plaster and walked to Yoash Street, near the houses of Teacher Vitkin and Mrs. Leipzig, and the parents of my friend Menahem who was killed next to me lived there. I came, and the father was digging a ditch around an ancient carob tree. Summer heat on all sides, and it was hot. The sea was a gigantic and silent and beautiful shining mass next to us. Max the Lunatic came to welcome me, and I approached the house, Menahem's mother came out, his father put an old hat on her I've remembered for years as a hat those teachers wore, he squinted from the sun and said, "Oh, Yoram," stressing the first syllable like Sarah my mother, and I said to him, "Greetings, Yosef," and to Menahem's mother, whom I wanted to know how much I loved Menahem, I said we had fought together and they had shot at us and there were vultures and crows and we played dead and they thought we were dead and they were bored and they shot us for no reason and Menahem was shot next to me from a bullet that was apparently aimed at me and I felt his blood flowing on me. Menahem's mother gave me a long look full of hate and said to her husband—she didn't talk to me directly despite years of niceness and acquaintance and intimate conversations of how to help Menahem and how you had to wear bathing suits, I had known her since I was eight years old—and she said, "That's Yoram, Yoraaaaaaaaaaam," she blurted out with bitter contempt, "the sweet son of teacher Sarah, tell me, Yosef," her voice was filled with an ancient righteous scathing rage, and she looked at me again but she said to her husband, "Too bad Menahem isn't coming to Yoram's mother now, to Sarah the licensed teacher, with Moshe his funny father from the museum with his music, instead of him coming here, why did it happen like that, why didn't it happen the other way around?"

The driver left. Music was coming from one of the rooms. We waited for the head nurse. I thought, this is the last stop, I don't want the future, and I'm blind with love, I believe there's nothing to believe in. No nobility in human beings. Fish eats fish. I'm neither a pessimist nor an optimist. I have to get better and that scares me. Sickness is a certain kind of escape and rest. You're a floor tile. You're a stone they treat any way they want. You have no wants of your own. You don't decide anything. You're in Paradise. There's a God who decides for you. You're wiped out. You're robbed of a shadow. Perforations and perforations and a twisted body that doesn't work as a body. You don't have to plan. Tomorrow will be like yesterday. Everything's organized.

In rehabilitation you don't choose either. Everything is managed like a list of equipment. You don't do the planning, and there's a desiccated, moldy, continuing present, neat and clean, and Galina, the beautiful head nurse, told me, "This isn't like a hospital. Here you get the tools to recover. If you want. But if you don't, nothing will help you and you'll stay here until you decide to recover. Success depends on you, because you didn't come here extinct but as someone who came out of that condition. Please, fight!" She went out and I looked at the window and saw what I would know later is the hospice for the terminally ill beyond the bend. Maybe I should have been there. To finish in the most beautiful place in the hospital grounds, and I had a window. I looked at it. My feet were cold, trying to run away from this place. But they were also afraid to run away. There was a head doctor here and four women doctors and nurses and caretakers, and if my heart pounded, somebody recorded that immediately. In rehabilitation, I suddenly understood what happened to me. How I was sick. I understood that I was apathetic. That most of the time I was spaced out on drugs and so most of what I remember was hallucination, but the hallucination apparently saved me.

The head nurse came back and very graciously taught me the house rules and smiled sweetly. So the rest of the days of my life began. After long weeks of repeated and backbreaking efforts, I started walking with a walker and I learned to eat almost by myself, and ultimately, I parted from the doctors and the nurses and the caretakers and they took me home. I'm trying to remember now the months of death and sickness and rehabilitation, but I remember only in spurts. I don't know exactly where I was when all that happened, but it happened, and at the age of seventy-five I died and I started to live again.

# SHIMON

SHIMON IS SENT TO ME by the national insurance. A righteous man blameless in his generation, loyal, thick, not fat, over six feet tall, which is tall and not just for a Jew. He's much bigger than he really is. He also looks just like Gary Cooper among the eternal Jewish people. The same shy sweet smile on the body of a retired boxer. He always comes on time. Wearing size-fifteen black shoes. The cuffs of his trousers never go to his shoes. The space between the cuffs of his trousers and his shoes is always the same three or so inches, but I don't think he really measures. In summer he rings the doorbell at 7:27, and in winter at 7:58. When I open the door he stands a bit away, as if retreating in respect, and he always looks shy and says as if he's swallowing, "What's happening?" Always, "What's happening." Once I asked him "What happenings?" He didn't know what happenings and stood leaning back a little and asked, "What?" "Happenings," I said, and he said, "Yes, happenings."

Miranda hurries to give him a glass of orange juice and a chocolate bar, and I give him the sports section of the newspaper, and that's what he reads all day long. If he thinks I look ready to go out he refuses to drink the juice, even though a few times Miranda managed to persuade him and he drank. I hold onto him when I go down the four steps at the entrance, and on the sidewalk the two of us look more relaxed. I ask what happened yesterday and he, with variations, tells me abut the heart attack he thinks he had, and touches the right sight of his chest. I explain to him that most attacks begin on the left side, and he asks what happens when the pain begins on the right side, since I did say "most." Once I confessed to him that I did know one man whose heart was on the right side, and then Shimon said maybe his heart was also on the right side, and I answered that that case was rare and if that was also his case, they would have informed him by now.

Shimon worked as a porter, he was an assistant mechanic, worked in a factory, worked arranging displays in grocery stores for Tnuva, did various boring jobs, the shops he worked in gave him what he called robot work. So he worked taking care of cripples, that was easier, freer, and he had been walking with old people for ten years now. Shimon lives on four thousand shekels a month and says that's enough for him, but what really sustains him is the belief that one of these days he'll win the lottery he plays every week. When he doesn't win, he says, "I lost again." When asked what he'd do if he made a million, he has no answer. All week he thinks about the lottery as a kind of divine windfall, but not about what he'd get if he won.

As soon as we go out to the street, Shimon recovers and forgets his diseases and watches me and becomes much more self-assured. He leads me as if he were born to lead and he's got the biggest and driest steps I ever saw. He walks at a pace that he sees I bring with me in the morning from home, and even though every day I bring a different pace, he can recognize it with the wisdom of those who take out and bring in, like those who walk dogs, and he can listen to body language and hover invisibly, and take strong and sure care of himself.

Shimon isn't a great reader. After he kept asking, I gave him one of my books. About nine months passed, he said the book was interesting and he had already gotten to page eleven, but as for the people, something in him reads them with the intelligence of someone who never had to read books. In our first conversation, when he first came to me, I think he asked me what a writer does. He's no fool, Shimon. Maybe he doesn't read a lot, but he's no fool. And if he did ask, it may have been because he wanted to understand, not what a writer does, but how he does it, because he once asked how I know what and when to write, and if I plan things in advance, and I admit I didn't know what to reply and I was silent. What is nice in Shimon and so characteristic of him is that he respected that.

Shimon is a big man, forty-seven years old, born in Ramat Gan. He attended grammar school and a regular boarding school and then a religious boarding school in Pardes Hanna-Karkur. When I asked him if he swam in the sea he said he hadn't yet. He explained that he used to swim when he was a child, with his father, but that had been thirty-some years ago and now he's alone. He loves to walk to the seashore in the evening, a walk he takes so he can fall asleep afterward.

Shimon was never abroad, even though once he thought of going to New York because he heard he had a relative there. He investigated and they told him he'd have to fill out a questionnaire in English and he didn't go. He doesn't have a driver's license because he never drove. When I asked if he'd like to drive he answered that he didn't have a car. He traveled very little in Israel, had almost never been in the Galilee or the Negev except on grammar school field trips or in the army as an airplane mechanic. In the army, as they say, they abused him, and after long questioning on my part, it turned out that it wasn't easy for him in the religious schools either, but he says he didn't really suffer because he doesn't take such things to heart. Shimon never says anything bad about anybody and recognizes everyone's right to get mad at him if they want. He walks with giant steps like a heavy but hovering animal, because there is a kind of sad heaviness about him, and that heaviness is full of a delightful lightness that won my heart.

When we started out, I stumbled and rested a lot, but after about a month I started flowing to life, and Shimon was patient and firm. Shimon is the most taciturn person I've known. His silence isn't the opposite of noise. He's silent in himself. He plays silence. He's silent as if silence were something tangible. His shyness is so nice and his long silence so noble that they're never a burden. Shimon, if such a thing can be said, has a proper silence. He's never restless. Proper or not. He isn't sad. He isn't depressed. Even when he tries to understand his many ailments he talks as if he's talking about somebody else. Shimon is the most solitary person I've met. He was married once, briefly, and he doesn't know many people; he has a persistent, fundamental isolation, and between us some basic misunderstanding prevails, but there isn't anyone I can talk with as with Shimon, and he also says I can talk with him the best.

After countless questions, I understand that he lives in the area of the old Central Bus Station, in what seems to me a kind of Tel Aviv hell, and he mutters, "As they say, fine, it's all cheap," and I ask what about massage parlors and whore houses and he mutters, "Yes, there are cheap women, yes." Never will he say "whores." He describes how the place is full of peddlers and shops with stolen goods and sex clubs, but he doesn't see them. He got a small apartment from a relative who loved him and who was, as they say, a good man, and when Shimon was a little boy he helped him and took him to live in his house and then left him the apartment.

Shimon gets home in the early evening, buys takeout food at the store on Keren HaYesod Street and goes home with the meal. He showers, puts the food in the microwave, and eats supper. That is, in fact, the only full meal he eats during the day. Afterward, he washes the plate or "does the dishes," as they say, and there are rental films on television and he chooses a film. It costs him eleven shekels a film, and he watches it and said, "As they say, I only see films I already saw before because then I don't have to start reading the subtitles again." Afterward, either at the end of the film or a little before, he, as they say, falls asleep and then he falls into bed.

One day, after five months, Shimon told me his father had written a book. I was amazed and asked him if he had read it and he answered, maybe, maybe yes, but a long time ago. I walked on a little and stumbled and he walked like someone who doesn't see a thing, but his hand reached out for me and he grabbed me hard and precisely and smiled, he always warns me to look down all the time. After a few questions, that same day and the following days, he told me his mother was Iraqi and his father was a Pole who was captured by the Germans, suffered, escaped from a concentration camp, went to Russia, found partisans, they took him to fight, he joined and fought in the Russian army in the difficult battles in Stalingrad and afterward they beat him because they discovered he was a Jew and he immigrated to the Land of Israel in an illegal-immigrant ship, Shimon didn't know which one, stayed in a transit camp in Cyprus, and then was interned in Atlit. He searched for his family and discovered that his brothers and parents were murdered and he felt that he had betrayed them, as they say, and he opened a little business making wallets. He made them by hand. They were in demand. He wrote a book about what had happened to him in the Holocaust, and the book was published by Yad Vashem, the Holocaust Memorial. He met his wife in Ramat Gan. She was much younger than him. As they say, he was an old man and she was a girl. He had terrifying dreams about everything he had gone through, and was sorry about his family, but his wife was impervious to his suffering, she was married off to him by her mother and he would yell in his sleep.

His wife's mother married her off to him because he was Ashkenazi and made wallets and made enough money and she didn't know what to do with him and didn't even know how to make an omelet. She did know, as they say, how to weep, and they had two children, Shimon and his brother. One day, Shimon's father came home and heard gasping. He ran and saw his wife sitting in the kitchen listening to the radio, he followed the direction of the yelling she didn't hear, and found Shimon almost dead under the hot water in the bathtub. They fought. Father loved me, says Shimon, but he was still in Stalingrad or with the Germans or searching for his relatives. Then they sent Shimon out of the city. His father wanted a religious son because maybe God would help him, and Shimon, who was big by then, didn't like Talmud and came home, but Father was busy and every afternoon he'd go out to play chess and played well, and he'd say that chess was like war but more peaceful. In chess, as they say, there isn't any death all day long.

Shimon didn't finish anything, he learned a little metalwork. One day he told me that a few years before he had taken care of a rabbi who lived near here on Ahad Ha'am Street, and the rabbi was fat, and Shimon would drag him. He had to sit a long time and wait for the end of the prayer and the rabbi was angry with him for not praying with him. Shimon said, "It must be awful to be sick in a hospital." I told him he must have worked with a lot of people who came from hospitals, and why didn't he ask the rabbi how it was to die. And Shimon said, "He's not like you, he didn't come back after he died, and I didn't see any other dead person who died before I met you." He asked how it was to come from there, I said to him, "From there you don't come, from there you flow."

Shimon, who isn't ashamed to talk about many things, doesn't understand the term "fraud." He never lies. He doesn't betray anyone. He doesn't speak evil and doesn't say a bad word about anyone. There's something hard and deep in him, and he looks dumb but he isn't. He's wise in his own way. He doesn't know evil tricks. He only watches movies on television, and I asked if he ever goes to the cinema and he said he would go but it's expensive.

Shimon doesn't look at anyone we pass by and he doesn't see all the gorgeous women walking on the boulevard in the morning, whom I, old man that I am, do see, and when I ask him why he doesn't look at the beautiful chicks, he smiles and blushes and says he doesn't look at them. Shimon likes things in their place. Likes them in their proper form and he knows they're out of his league.

Shimon asked me, "Say, Yoram, when you die, do you see death?" His body was shaking a little when he asked and I told him you don't see anything. Death is a kind of something that's nothing. I told him that, in English, they say I have nothing. That stunned him a little and he looked at me in amazement.

Shimon's greatest dream was to be a mailman, but, as he said, "I don't have a bike and I don't read names in English." He brought me his father's book after he searched for a copy for about a month, and when I was amazed that he didn't have the book and how come he needed so much time to find it, he was amazed at my amazement.

His father once told him to change his last name to Zelig, and so when I asked him for his full name, he said "Shimon Zelig." His father and mother got divorced. His mother married an Iraqi and had a daughter and Shimon lived with his father, who fell ill and then died, or as he says they say, "passed away." His mother separated from her husband and had been in the hospital for years. Once or twice a year, he goes to visit her. He has almost nothing to do with his brother and he has some cousins he sees now and then. He also used to have two friends. One was a fellow who did the same work he did, but he made him angry and the friend was offended, and the other one, Mr. B., died a few months ago at the age of eighty.

He said that B. had been in the Palmach and was a ladies' man, and didn't get married, and would, says Shimon, bring home girls from Jaffa and was constantly involved with those girls and with the Palmach and with Dado and Rabin and Ra'anana, who remained the important people in his life. He hadn't seen them since 1948, but they remained the rock of his existence. B. was coarse, fat, and sick, but he was afraid of examinations and lived near Shimon's house, and Shimon would buy him food and warm it up and they'd sit and watch films together and B. would tell about the battles of the Palmach in Jerusalem and about the widows there, most of whom were "cheap" and would run after him. When he got sick, Shimon took him to Ichilov and took care of him and watched him die, and he, despite the burden he was on Shimon, was the only person close to him.

Shimon told me, "Nobody ever talked with me, how do they call it, from the soul. Only you and your wife. I don't know such a thing." Shimon is solitary as a thorn. Today I'm his only friend. I wait for him in the morning as for the Messiah.


This is the route for our walk: we go up Luntz Street, pass by my daughter Naomi's apartment, come to Rothschild Boulevard, and turn right past the crossing on Hashmonaim Street. Shimon teaches me to wait until the cars pass by and I give them the right of way—those who run the red light honking their horn angrily, he doesn't even judge those barbarians, he asks me not to get angry, and to refrain, for my own good, from trying to teach the drivers to drive politely, because sometimes I argue with them and get mad, and then he smiles his shy smile and says, "Why argue with them? How will you win?"

Sometimes we get to the boulevard through Sheinkin Street. But the traffic signal at the corner of Sheinkin and Rothschild, they say, is the longest traffic signal in the

Western world, even though, honestly, not everyone who says that has really checked all the traffic signals in the Western world. And that traffic signal constitutes an eternal rock of contention, since if Tel Aviv is indeed the Zionist capital, that traffic signal is a black mark on its landscape. The people who stand at that traffic signal and wait for the light to change always and without exception get mad at it. They stand mad, curse, grumble, and look here and there and say more or less the same things. They say in a threatening voice that with such traffic signals, they'll leave Israel, they say you have to yell at the mayor that nobody does anything about it, and anyway what kind of state is this with a traffic signal like that.

Shimon is nice and indifferent to the traffic signal. While waiting for the light to change, he rests from the five minutes of walking here and looks at the sports section, but his hand is constantly stretched out to my shoulder to protect me. After the light changes we cross and go on the boulevard and start walking west. On the boulevard, you feel a thin breeze coming through Sheinkin from the sea. In the morning, the boulevard is shrouded with magic at the tops of the beautiful trees, the old houses on either side are still in shade and shower a bittersweet bliss of morning. Even in summer.

On the left side, at the corner of Sheinkin, stands a three-story house that was restored for about eight years.

Ever since the work was completed it has stood empty. Under the house you see something like a big garage, the house is completely air-conditioned, it has all the appurtenances of a palace, it just doesn't have tenants. Shimon once asked me why there are no tenants in the building, and I told him that I had once checked out of curiosity and learned that the owner wasn't interested in selling or renting apartments separately but wanted somebody to buy the entire building. Shimon asked why they don't buy. I answered that if he had three and a half million dollars, that house could be his. Shimon thought a little and said, "No, I don't have it."

At twenty-five to eight, we come to the Balfour Street corner of Rothschild. There is the beautiful white stone house by the architect Berlin, one of the most beautiful in Tel Aviv, but of course they murdered it and added a story and destroyed its nature, and kitty-corner from it stands an empty four-story building, you see it was once beautiful but now it's run-down, the windowpanes are shattered and the windows are covered with announcements and old newspapers, and on the roof of the house, on a small concrete crown, it says "1926." The house has no glory like other houses in the area, but it mustn't be destroyed because houses like that have to be preserved. The crown is like the tombstone I saw when I celebrated my birthday in the hospital. That one said 1930, and here it says "1926." Four years difference.

I lived in that house, at 88 Rothschild, in the first three years of my life. Sarah my mother held me in her arms wrapped in a thin blanket and somehow I know it was blue, and she walked from Freund Hospital on Yehuda Ha-Levi Street near number three, and it was morning then, said Sarah my mother, and Moshe my father waited for her, she said, even though sometimes she recalled that he didn't wait, and when she recalled that he didn't wait, her face became sad in the version of the eternal forsaken woman. I came to that house when I was less than a week old during a heat wave in early May, or to be precise, at the beginning of the month of Iyar, and there's a photo that shows me standing on the porch facing the boulevard with trees that were then small and low, and I seem hidden behind the small pillars that look like paper cutouts, and I'm peeping out through the spaces between them.

It's important for me to see that house in the morning because when I see it I feel comfortable and I know I'm alive, and on the day the house is destroyed I believe I shall die. Shimon isn't a romantic and so he says, "So that's your childhood home, as they say?" And I tell him yes, and he says, "So maybe you won't die, they're repairing it now, look, and, as they say, a destroyed house, a dead man." When I ask Shimon who says that, he answers, "My father would." Shimon always quotes. He doesn't put himself into any story. He doesn't commit himself to anything and it's all as they say.

After we cross Maze Street, we come to a café in a kiosk, and only those who come to it know its name and it's always buzzing. Even in the morning it's a variegated club of people who make it a refuge from their connection to humanity outside, and when it's cold—a rare event—they cling to the wall of the buffet, and they're all immune to the rain or cold and if the situation is especially bad, they gather around a heater outside, even in the rain, and manage to ignore it. When they're hot they almost hide from the sun and during the day, the customers change and a few steps away from that café there's another café.

The second café is exactly like the first but it's always empty. In both of them, the same coffee and the same sandwiches are served, in both of them you can read the same newspapers, and they're no more than twenty yards apart. When I asked, the regulars told me that the first one had existed for years and they were used to it and met there, at 7:40 in the morning those same people sit there on the benches of the boulevard or on a few high bar stools, always the same people, and drink and eat and read the newspapers or let their dogs play together. Since we always pass by there at the same time, nineteen or twenty minutes to eight, except Friday, you can set your watch by it. But these days when everyone sees the time on their cell phones while hearing their favorite songs and can even take pictures of their grandchildren, and the cell phone does everything but make coffee, it's not fashionable to wear watches, as in the past. And yet, our passing by them, I think, gives them a certain kind of confidence.

One of them always reads the inside pages of the paper, a plump woman who used to walk on the boulevard as if she were shot out of a cannon sits serenely and smiles and drinks coffee in a cup the way we used to do in our youth before they started drinking coffee in a mug in Israel, and sweet and funny Toveleh, queen of women's clothes, sits there holding court, and she always calls out, "Hello, Yoram," and pronounces my name like Sarah my mother, and that makes my day just as at night I'm nourished by the way the beautiful Yonit Levi says with a shy charm, "among other things," and Shimon hears what I say about the watches and about Yonit Levi, and says, "As they say, a regular schedule, that's an important thing."

We go on walking and pass by dogs with sleepy-morning human beings and a few old people walking with brand-name exercise shoes and young men running with earphones stuck to their ears and young women hurrying to work holding hot coffee in paper mugs, and one poor dog with three legs and a handsome and sweet woman even in the morning, and we get to the corner of Nakhmani Street. The trees planted in beds are all Israeli trees, and they come together at the top and almost create a vault like a medieval cathedral, or a green tunnel, and the cultivated, twined trees, their blossoms are interwoven into one another and among them are twisted shapes of branches growing down and up, laced together like statues that look like a mixture of stumps and arms. We go on and cross Nakhmani Street and sometimes we have to stop and wait for the light to change.

After Nakhmani, there's a path of trees without benches. On one of our first walks on the boulevard, I thought that, in the order of their planting, in the way they grew, the trees had something sublime, strength and silence, and they curve into and around themselves and are full of tendrils. The branches of the twined trees, sucking the trunks like a sort of local sculpture of God, if He would deign to come down to the boulevard.

In the summer, a beautiful girl would come to the flower-bed between Nakhmani and Hillel Yaffe Streets, a Russian, from her Slavic-looking face, and make charming leaps on her skateboard. She didn't speak, didn't see any of us who were looking at her, would delight me with the beauty of her tricks, but because that's not something you do or that Shimon remembers from his childhood, he doesn't see.

At a quarter to eight, at the corner of Hillel Yaffe Street, I tend to turn my face to number 55 at the corner. In that house, the Sadeh family once lived. The father was a licensed ear doctor and the son still is. The building is one of the most beautiful in Tel Aviv, in the style of the 1920s, that eclectic style I love and that reminds me of my childhood dreams of being in a beautiful and distant land. There was something enchanting about the building, and even though today it's crumbling here and there, it's still dignified.

Once I pointed to the beautiful palm tree growing next to the three stories of the house, I showed Shimon the tree that had apparently been planted when the house was built and today its crest reaches the third story, but whoever planted it didn't imagine that it was too close to the building and they didn't know it would persist in growing so close, and it has bowed over like a loyal dog and instead of growing straight like every decent tree, it's grown close to the house and the balconies and looks like a bow. I told Shimon, "A tree like a bow is rare in our city."

Behind it stood the house of the Moyal family, with the fireplace of Armenian tiles from Jerusalem—blue with miniature olive trees painted on them—and in the living rooms the floor tiles were of terra cotta. Next to it was my uncle Joseph's house, which was destroyed long ago and on its rubble they built a narrow three-story building that looked like a public pissoir, and I didn't have any more family left on the boulevard where I once knew almost everybody. My uncle Joseph must have been upset that the company that built on the rubble of his house decided that the sign outside would be only in English, and his wife, big Sarah, who died a long time ago, left the property and the house in her will to the granddaughter or grandson who would come live in Israel, because her son lived in the United States for many years. Only one granddaughter came, lived here for a year, inherited the house, sold it, and went back to Pittsburgh.

Around the corner of Ramhal Street, every day we passed a pretty young woman walking with a murderous mastiff, and she looked as if the dog was some old lover of hers, and she apparently hated people. Once I asked her what kind of dog that was because I had forgotten a lot of things when I was in the hospital, and she said, "Fuck off."

At the corner of Shadal Street, when we first started walking together, they started building a giant First International Bank building. As we passed by there, I would lift my face to the giant crane for a moment and say, "Since yesterday they built another story, they're working here as in America, fast and thorough." And Shimon would stare at me in wonder, maybe he thought I was making a big deal out of something so small. So what if they build a story a day? So what if the construction grows and people work and trucks enter and at the top of the crane sits a person who looks so small and steers the crane, "That's a building they're building," he says, "as they say, it has to be built." And one morning, near Shadal Street, near the International Bank that was bursting up, I saw Shimon blush. He said that yes, he once had a story. Once he knew a woman who was thirty-eight years old and was with her. It was nice.

217

She was a good woman. She had a dog. She worked in a flower shop. He described her very lovingly. She got sick and died of cancer.

After Yavne Street, we always pass by the Romanian couple, or at least they speak Romanian, walking arm in arm. They're old and thin and always engaged in a lively conversation, but they aren't old in their old age and they walk fast and erect, as if it's important to them to feel they're still here and together, lest something bad befall afterward, and there's an incipient panic in their faces. Behind them skips a rather ugly little dog, they look at us and we look at them, or more precisely, I look at them, because Shimon sees almost nothing on the boulevard except what I talk about or what he recognizes or remembers. A few months later, they pass by us without the dog. The next day, too. And we met them again a few days later and the dog wasn't there. I understood that the dog had died. On their faces I saw a kind of sadness that hadn't been there before. I stared at the woman and she nodded her head as if to say thanks, and I wanted to tell her that I understood very well what it is to mourn for the death of a dog, but I was afraid to speak because I didn't know if the dog had indeed died.

The mornings are beautiful in summer and in winter, and we go on walking to Allenby and then we turn and go back through the whole boulevard and come to the end of Marmorek Street. On Marmorek we turn right, pass by

Bank Leumi and Café Marmorek, pass the small parking lot, turn right again and stop at Café Cremieux, on the corner of Karmiya and Bilu Streets, across from the park that has recently been revived and looks very nice. In Café Cremieux, my table is waiting and I drink some orange juice and eat a croissant with orange marmalade and drink coffee, and Shimon orders a big cup of instant coffee with milk and glances at the sports page I give him. He's the last one who drinks Elite instant coffee and feels strange with the American coffee and the cappuccino and the small espresso. Afterward, Shimon walks me home and at the house, I shake his big hand and thank him. He smiles his sweet smile and I go into the house, to begin the rest of the days of my life.

# EPILOGUE

I WANT TO DIE on a warm day that isn't hot and isn't cold, not in a heat wave and not in the rain, to make it easy for those who'll come. I give up on a funeral. I want them to cremate my body. You can do such a thing today. I don't want to take up space in any earth, not even on a kibbutz, certainly not in a Jewish cemetery with bodies tossed into pits, but if so, let them be gracious to me and bury me in Trumpeldor, but I want Miranda to be buried next to me when her time comes, and she isn't Jewish and isn't circumcised and if I'm buried there maybe they can convert her body and bury her next to me.

My ashes will take on a song and come back with your Messiah to heaven and I will throw a rock at God, whether God exists and is black or not. I shall go into the ICU in heaven and come back to the hallucinations that were my portion while I was sick, because there I had a richer life than what I have here today. And now, as an old man with cancer and a hernia and a destroyed belly, I leave you.

TEL AVIV, JUNE, 2007

## ABOUT THE AUTHOR

YORAM KANIUK (1930–2013) was born in Tel Aviv and took part in Israel's War of Independence in 1948. A painter, journalist, and theater critic, he was best known as a novelist. His twenty-nine books include *The Acrophile* (1960), *Himmo, King of Jerusalem* (1968), *Adam Resurrected* (1971), *Rockinghorse* (1977), *Confessions of a Good Arab* (1984), *His Daughter* (1988), *Commander of the Exodus* (1999), *The Last Jew* (2006), *1948* (2012), and *Between Life and Death*, and have been translated into twenty languages. He won the Bialik Prize, the French Prix des Droits de l'Homme, the Israeli President's Prize, the Newman Prize, and the Sapir Prize for Literature.

## ABOUT THE TRANSLATOR

BARBARA HARSHAV has been translating works from French, German, Hebrew, and Yiddish for over twenty years and has currently published over forty books of translation, including works of poetry, drama, fiction, philosophy, economics, sociology, and history.